Even More Tales

of a

Highland Minister

by

Rev. Iain Ramsden

Book 3

This book is dedicated to my lovely wife, Jo, for all her help, inspiration and support.

I am grateful to family members and a number of kind-hearted friends for their positivity and encouragement.

With special thanks to my good friend John Malcolm (aka PC Bookem) for all his thoughts, ideas and invaluable input.

"Tha mi fadah nad chomain"

'I am very grateful to you'

ISBN: 978-1-917425-38-4

Even more Tales of a Highland Minister

This is the third book in the series which continues the exploits of the Reverend Colin Campbell, a young Church of Scotland Minister who, although being born and bred in Glasgow, fell in love with the beautiful and remote Island of Rhua, which is off the West Coast of Scotland, where faith, fun and folklore are interwoven like threads of gold and silver, through the fabric of everyday life.

But more than that, he fell in love with the delightful Lorna MacDonald when visiting the Island to conduct the funeral service of his maternal Grandmother, Mrs Martha McGillivray, some months before.

Life for Colin, was never to be the same.

Book 1 gives us an introduction to the many characters and begins the storyline.

Book 2 builds on book 1. We get to know the characters better and see more hi-jinks, plus a very 'special' day.

Book 3 is a series of short stories which are full of humour, folklore and beliefs of the Islands, some of which remain to this very day.

All through these books, you will see the fun, faith and friendships which bonds the hardy Islanders as they encourage and support each other in their daily lives on these remote, yet fascinating and beautiful Islands.

Many of the tales and incidents in these books are taken from my own personal experience or events I have seen and heard, while others may well have happened to somebody, somewhere.

Anyone with even the slightest knowledge of the Highlands and Islands of Scotland will recognise the humour and the antics of the local characters – with a good dram of poetic license for added flavour!

Set in the late 1940's, early 1950's, those of a 'certain age' will readily identify with a simpler way of life.

So, make yourself a cup of tea or coffee *(or perhaps something stronger),* find yourself a comfy seat and be transported back to a different time and a very different place.

Gabh Tlachd!
Enjoy!

A bit about the Author

Rev Iain Ramsden is a retired Church of Scotland Minister from a small village among the hills of Argyll and is now living in Glasgow. He served in the Royal Navy and then on the road squads and Forestry around the Highlands and Islands of Scotland before being called into the Ministry, serving 2 Congregations on the Black Isle for 15 years.

He was brought up listening to tales of Scottish folklore, Mythology and ancient stories of banshees, fairies, kelpies, mermaids, selkies, witches and much more at his Highland Grandmother's knee - who is now resting in peace in Appin Cemetery.

The Chapters

Chapter 1

The Minister and the Secret Admirer…

It had been three months since the wedding and Colin and Lorna were enjoying married life very much.

Attendances at the church were growing and Colin was enjoying getting to know his parishioners.

After Colin discovered that Callum McLeod's mischievous suggestion of naming their the Croft, 'Marag dhubh' actually translated as, 'Black Pudding', Lorna suggested they should name their home, 'An Caladh' (*ann-calla*) which means, 'The Haven/Heaven or Retreat).'

Callum laid low for a few weeks until the dust had settled.

*

It was a normal Monday morning and Colin and Lorna were having a lazy morning, it being the Ministers' designated day off after a hectic week and a busy Sunday Service.

Lorna slipped on her dressing gown and opened the front door to take in the small urn of milk that Ruaraidh McRae, the milkman, aka 'Ruaraidh fear-bainne' (Rory the milkman) left for them every Monday and Thursday mornings.

The urn of milk was there as expected, but there was also a small brown paper bag on the step, on which were written the words 'To the Meenister,' and there was also a strong smell of Lavender coming off the bag.

Lorna called Colin through to the kitchen saying, "Colin, will you come and look at this." He wandered through as Lorna was opening the paper bag. "What is it?" Colin asked.
"Scones!"
"Scones?"

"Aye, scones!" Lorna said, "and from a secret admirer by the looks of it."

"Well, I never," Colin was as puzzled as Lorna.

"And whoever left them is a lover of Lavender, here, smell the bag," and she held out the bag for Colin to take a sniff.

"Gosh, that's strong enough to knock out a Heiland coo! Whoever can it be from?"

"Aye, that's what *I* was wondering!" Lorna looked suspiciously at Colin.

"Well, don't look at me! I've no idea," Colin said defensively.

Lorna wasn't happy.

"I bet it's thon Mrs McVitie, the lady who sits in the front pew, you know, the one with the purple rinse and the squint. She fairly reeks of Lavender, you can smell it at a hundred yards!" Colin laughed, "Surely not, she's 90 if she's a day!"

"Aye well, maybe she likes the young men!" Lorna said mischievously. "I see I'll have to keep my eye on you, Romeo!"

A few days later, 'Murdo the Post' brought the Post to the Manse as usual. There were the usual bills, and there was also a small pink envelope, simply addressed to 'The Meenister, The Manse' and smelling strongly of Lavender.

Colin met Murdo at the door and as he handed over the post, Murdo commented on the strong smelling envelope. "My goodness Meenister, there's a fair whiff off that letter! It smells stronger than Oban Pier! It'll linger in my van for a week or two to be sure, the wife will be getting suspicious! Would it be from a secret admirer, Meenister?"

Colin looked at Murdo, "Why do you say that? Do you know something?"

"Mercy no Meenister, but why would someone send the Meenister a parcel reeking of Lavender?"

At this point Lorna had joined them at the front door. "Good morning Murdo, how is Mrs McRae keeping?"

"Och she is just the usual, thank you for asking. She says she has a full time job keeping her eyes on me!" he laughed.

"Aye, you men!" Lorna smiled, "You certainly keep us ladies on our toes!"

"Aye, I see what you mean," and Murdo nodded towards the pink envelope."

Colin handed her the strong smelling envelope. "What's this Colin?" she asked. He had been hoping to put it in the dustbin before Lorna could see it as he didn't want her to be upset by this second 'token of affection' from his unknown admirer.

"Och it's just someone's idea of a joke, sweetheart."

"Not much of a joke if you ask me," added Murdo.

"Thank you Murdo, we'll take it from here," Colin added, thinking that Murdo's opinion wasn't helping matters at all, and he closed the door.

Lorna and Colin sat at the kitchen table, staring at the letter. "Well, open it then," said Lorna.

Colin felt a slight chill in the air as he slowly slit open the envelope.

"Well, what does it say?"

Colin handed it over and Lorna and she read it out.

"Dearest Meenister," it started, *"You are the best Meenister we have had for many years…"*

"Aye, the <u>only</u> Minister they've had in many years," Colin said.

It continued… *"The way you explain the Scriptures is just sublime and your prayers are like a hairy blanket that wraps around my heart and keeps it warm – and it is true to say that we never knew what sin was until you came here.*

I hope you enjoyed the scones."

"Goodness me! what does she mean by, *'we never knew what sin was until you came here!?'*" Lorna said angrily.

"Don't worry sweetpea, it'll be a joke. Aye, that's what it is, a silly joke." Colin tried to convince Lorna but had to admit that he wasn't fully convinced of it himself.

"She must mean that Sermon I gave a few weeks ago when I explained the dangers of how sin can creep up on us," Colin said, hoping to pacify Lorna.

"Aye, maybe..." Lorna was not convinced.

Within ten minutes of leaving the Manse, 'Murdo the Post' was in Mr Ali's convenience store where he 'accidentally' let slip about the Minister receiving a pink, heavily scented letter, and the 'mystery of the anonymous scones.'

The ladies of the village were shocked to hear this latest revelation regarding their new Minister.

"Well, well, it's the devil's work to be sure," said Mrs McCrimmond, the Free Church Minister's wife. "The sins of the flesh are the weakness of men, you only have to think of Samson and Delilah."

"Aye," the ladies shook their heads in deference to Mrs McCrimmond's biblical knowledge, while at the same time not seeing what the Meenister and a bag of scones had to do with Samson and Delilah.

"Do you think he has a fancy woman?" one lady speculated.

"And him with such a lovely wife in young Lorna MacDonald too," said another shaking her head.

Word soon got round the Island, and the state of Colin and Lorna's marriage was a matter of hot gossip among those who were willing to spread rumour and tittle-tattle without knowing all the facts, but as someone once said, *"Why let the facts spoil a good story?"*

Colin and Lorna were completely unaware of the rumours going around and were happily getting on with life as if nothing was wrong, which was, of course, the true version of events. Over the next few weeks an array of scones, pancakes, soda bread and tray bakes mysteriously appeared at the Manse door, each wrapped in a brown paper bag.

The temperature in the Manse was becoming decidedly chillier as the weeks passed.

Each Sunday morning Colin scanned the congregation for some sign of who the secret admirer might be, as did Lorna. However, no-one seemed to stand out as a furtive scarlet woman harbouring a secret passion for men of the cloth.

Every new hat, each new dress, handbag or hairdo was noticed and catalogued in the mind of Lorna under the heading, 'Possible marriage wrecker.'

Colin, however, was oblivious to all the subtleties of womanly wiles. The smiles, the prolonged handshakes after church, the new stockings and the fancy coloured hair nets, went right over his head.

Then, one Sunday morning, while he was in the middle of a particularly eloquent sermon, he spotted an elderly lady sitting at the back of the church.

That, in itself, wasn't unusual as the majority of the congregation of Kinlochmhor Parish Church were elderly ladies who liked to sit at the back.

She smiled at Colin and every few minutes she would give him a little wave and a nod of the head.

"Oh my goodness," Colin thought, "It's her, the secret admirer!"

For a brief moment he lost the thread of his sermon and stood there in silence, with a dazed look on his face. "It's her!" he mumbled to himself, "It's her! I can see her!" and a shiver ran down his spine.

Some of the congregation became anxious, others giggled nervously and a few hadn't noticed that Colin had stopped speaking as they were busy counting the panes of glass on the church windows.

Lorna looked up and gave him a, *"Are you alright?"* look but he had momentarily lost the plot.

The whole episode had only lasted for less than a minute, but for Lorna and the congregation, the silence seemed so much longer.

John McRae, the Presenter, called up, "Are you alright Meenister!?"

John's words seemed to stir Colin from his trance-like state.

"Er…Yes… I'm fine John, thank you…." and he looked around and realized that the whole of the church was staring at him.

"Yes, I'm alright… I just…. I just … er… thought I saw someone I wasn't expecting to see…." and he slowly got back on track.

Mrs Gordon shouted, "Oh mercy, it's the second sight that he has, Praise the Lord!" The congregation nodded to each other and gazed up at Colin with a new level of respect.

At the end of the service, the congregation swarmed around Colin, shaking his hand and asking if he was alright.

"It is the second sight that you have Meenister!" Mrs McKillop said, and the others all agreed.

Colin was touched by their concern but shrugged off the episode, saying, "I think I might have a cold coming on."

He looked around the church but the wee smiley lady at the back was nowhere to be seen. Colin doubted his own sanity for a moment, had a sweet old lady *really* been smiling and waving at him from the back of the church, or was it all in his imagination?
On the way home after the service, Lorna asked Colin what on earth had happened and he explained what he had seen, or what he *thought* he had seen.

When Lorna saw how it was affecting Colin, she became angry. "For goodness sake! Whoever is playing these silly games needs to be stopped before some real damage is done! I'm going to speak to PC Malcolm and see what he can do."
"Och, there's no need to bother Bookem, I'm sure it's all a harmless misunderstanding."
"Harmless? It's games that she is playing, and I'll not let her ruin our marriage, not if I can help

it!" When they got home, Lorna picked up the phone and called the Police Station.

Within 15 minutes there was a knock on the Manse door. It was PC Bookem with note pad and sharpened pencil at the ready.

"Come away in John," Lorna said to Bookem. "We're just having a cup of tea, will you take one yourself? Four sugars if I remember correctly? Or perhaps a wee 'sensation' to keep out the cold?"

"Not for me, if you don't mind, I never drink while on duty." Colin was in the living room and nearly choked on his cup of tea when he heard that.

PC Bookem was well known for taking a dram 'just to be sociable' on just about *any* occasion.

"Aye four sugars but don't be stirring it, it makes it too sweet.

I like to keep a clear head when I'm on a case, but thank you all the same."

Lorna thought that this was hardly a 'case' but called Colin through to the kitchen anyway.

"Are you okay Meenister?" Bookem asked Colin.

" I heard that you took a wee turn in church this morning. They're saying it was the second sight that came upon you."

Colin was surprised that the news of his 'blip' in church had travelled so quickly. "Och, it was nothing John, just a wee bug working on me, I think."

"Well, we'd better get on with the case, can't be sitting around blethering when there's perpetractors at large.

Now, what is the incident you want investigated?"

Bookem was in 'official Police mode' as he opened his notebook, licked the end of his pencil and was poised to take notes to assist him in catching the perpetrator. All he needed were statements from any witnesses and he would be off on the trail, like a well trained bloodhound on the scent of an international criminal.

Colin thought this was all getting a bit out of hand. "It's nothing serious John, probably just a silly misunderstanding, I'm sure."

"I'll be the judge of that Meenister, and by the way, please call me PC Malcolm when I am on official duty."

"Oh, yes of course John, sorry, PC Malcolm." Colin looked over at Lorna who was struggling to keep a straight face.

It had been a while since Bookem had a 'case' to investigate. The mystery of Mrs McLean's missing cat, 'Maeve,' had been a real challenge.

All clues led to old Mr McGill having taken poor Maeve away one night, but after obtaining numerous statements and some 'under cover' work, it was established that Maeve had actually ran off with a half wild ginger tom cat called Piseag (Peeshak) and they had set up home in the hill above the village and were now the proud parents of four bonny ginger kittens.

Then there was the, 'Curious Case of the Holy Bothan.' It was a case that he would rather forget but the local 'lads' were sure to remind him every now and then. But that's another story for another day.

Bookem took copious notes as Colin and Lorna explained all the circumstances around the secret admirer, the scones and the notes – and of course, the incident in the church.
Lorna wasn't sure if the two were connected but thought it best to give Bookem all the facts and let him sort it out.
"Now, can you tell me what this lady in the church looked like Meenister?" Bookem asked, pencil at the ready.
"Well, she was a small lady with silver hair, red cheeks, and she wore a pair of round rimmed glasses."

"That's good Meenister, is there anything else?" Colin thought for a moment and added, "Oh yes, she wore her hairnet at a jaunty angle!"

Bookem furiously wrote down all the details and then went through the list in his notebook.

"Silver hair, rosy cheeks – round glasses – and hair net – at – jaunty – angle," he said slowly to make sure he had got it all down correctly.

"Every investigation rests on good note keeping," Bookem always told the young police cadets who occasionally came over to Rhua for, 'Life on a remote island' training.'

"Is that everything now, you haven't forgotten anything?"
"Oh yes, did I mention the strong smell of Lavender on the notes and paper bags with the scones?"

This seemed to peak Bookem's interest. "Mmm, scones *and* lavender you say? That could be significant if it comes to a 'line up.' And he wrote more notes in his wee black book.

"It looks like you have been having quite a time of it, but never fear, I have it all in hand. I'll soon have the culprint apprehended and brought to justice before you can say, *Bonny Ballachulish!*"

Colin and Lorna could see that Bookem was taking this 'case' seriously, perhaps a little *too* seriously.

"Well, if there's nothing else, I'll be on my way. 'Strike before the trail goes cold' is my motto!" and he rose and made for the door.
Colin and Lorna thanked him for coming so promptly and shut the door behind him, but within a few minutes there was a knock at the door, it was Bookem and he had a puzzled look on his face.
"Did you forget something?" Colin asked.
"No, but I was thinking about that lady you described, and I'm sure it reminds me of someone." Bookem scratched his head and then, as if a light bulb had been suddenly switched on, he said, "I've got it!"
"Got what?" Lorna asked.
"I know who that lady is. At first I thought it was a pigment of my imagination but now I remember.

The rosy cheeks, the glasses and the smiling face, yes, it's quite uncanny. She had the 'second sight' you know."

He smiled and began to walk away shaking his head.

"Who? Who is it?" Colin was getting exasperated now.

"Oh yes, sorry. It's Mrs Martha McGillivray, your dear departed grandmother! She always dressed up in her Sunday best for church. If you were seeing her then it must be the 'second sight' that you have inherited from her, Meenister.

But I don't remember her ever making the scones. Oatcakes and Soda Bread were her speciality. Oh well, better be off."

Colin closed the door and shook his head saying, "Me, the second sight? I've lived all my life in Glasgow, how would I know anything about that? I've heard of seeing double but only after a glass or two of dry sherry!"

As Bookem walked back down the hill to the Police Station a lady from the church carrying a small brown paper bag, was coming up towards him. "Good morning Constable Malcolm," she said as she passed by.

"Good morning Mrs McNeill, lovely day," Bookem replied.

It was then that he became aware of a strong smell of Lavender. He turned and called, "Mrs McNeill, can I have word?"

After a short chat, Mrs McNeill was horrified to learn that she had been the cause of the bad feeling in the Manse.

"Oh, dear me, I was just giving some of my home baking to the Meenister and his wife. I do a bake twice a week and I always make too much. I remember him saying that he missed his Aunty in Glasgow's home baking."

"Well, that was very thoughtful of you Mrs McNeill but perhaps you would be better not to make so much baking in future," suggested Bookem.

Mrs McNeill was mortified, but she also felt a tinge of excitement. *"Imagine! I'm the 'scarlet woman' they were all talking about, and I didn't even know it!*

Whoever would have though, me, a scarlet woman? What would my Angus say if he were to find out?" With a twinkle in her eye she hurried home to tell Angus the latest news.

Bookem explained it all to Colin and Lorna who was pleased it was just a well intended mix up. Colin felt a wee bit disappointed – it had been quite nice to think that he had a secret admirer.

Colin put his arms around Lorna and gave her a hug." What was that for?" Lorna asked, smiling.

"Just because..." and he kissed her on the forehead.

There were no more scones, pancakes or home-bakes left at the Manse door after that day, much to the delight of Lorna and the disappointment of Colin.

Lorna was happy now that all the loose ends had been tied up. it had all been just a silly misunderstanding.

It was a happy ending to a difficult few weeks.

Colin continued to see his dear Grandmother smiling at him from the back of the church every Sunday morning – but far from troubling him, he found her presence rather comforting.

PC Bookem was pleased with his 'crime busting skills.' Another case had been solved!

"Wait until Sergeant Galbraith hears of my detective work, my promotion surely won't be long in coming now," he said to himself as he walked back to the Police Station whistling the catchy Gaelic song, 'Gaol ise Gaol i.' (*She's my love, my love is she*).

He poured himself a bumper sized dram, held it up and said, 'Slainte Mhath' and downed it in one gulp. Well, he wouldn't want it to evaporate before he could finish it, now would he?

*

Foot Note : <u>*The 'Second sight'*</u> *is the exceptional psychic 'gift' of prophetic visions, premonitions and an ability to see beyond this world. It is traditionally believed to be a natural inborn ability of mind running in certain families in the Western*

Highlands and Islands of Scotland. Almost every village or area would have had someone who had 'the gift of the second sight.'

Chapter 2

The Minister and the Tinker's Curse...

It was a lovely sunny Monday morning in the small village of Kinlochmhor, and the Rev Colin Campbell had been out for a ride around the island on his motorbike.

He had been born and bred in Glasgow and since moving up to Rhua he never ceased to be amazed at the breathtaking natural beauty and splendour of the Highlands and Islands of the West coast of Scotland.

He was humming his favourite Psalm, Psalm 121 "I to the hills will lift mine eyes," as he pulled up outside Mr Ali's general store.

A small group of ladies were standing outside the shop catching up on the latest village 'news' as Colin came to a stop beside them. He gave the throttle a twist, giving the engine a final roar as he switched off.

His, "Good morning ladies, what a glorious morning," was met with a stony silence that spoke volumes as they sniffed and filed into the shop.

'*Oh dear,*' he thought, '*it looks like I'm not the flavour of the day,*' and entered the shop after them.

"Oh it's yourself Meenister, come away in," said Mr Ali with an almost flawless Highland accent, except, that is, for a slight hint of Bengali. "And what can I be getting for you today?"

"I'm just in for a pan loaf and a couple of packets of Custard Creams."

"Of course, Meenister, I'll not be a minute." Mr Ali hurried off to get Colins' messages.

The ladies were chatting in the corner of the shop and four pairs of eyes were focused on Colin, looking him up and down.

"How are you all this fine morning, ladies?" Colin said as he attempted to engage them in conversation once more.

"Oh, it's yourself Meenister, we didn't recognise you without your dog collar," showing obvious disapproval of his attire which consisted of a leather jacket, denim jeans, open necked shirt and leather boots.

"Oh yes, Mrs Grant, Monday is my day off after the stress and strains of a Sunday." Colin said with a smile.
"I would have thought that doing the Lord's work on the Sabbath day would not be a strain for a man of the cloth!" Mrs Grant replied as the other ladies agreed and tut-tutted.
"Of course, Mrs Grant … that isn't what I meant…I…er…"
"Huh, the very idea, come on ladies, it's time for our prayer meeting with Mrs Killmennie, we'll get our messages on the way back," and they left Mr Ali's shop with more tutting.

"Oh dear, Meenister, I think you've upset the ladies, but that's not hard to do!" Mr Ali laughed and handed Colin his messages.
"Yes, so it seems, oh well, I live to fight another day. How much do I owe you, Mr Ali?"
"Take them with my compliments – and don't you worry about Mrs Grant, she thrives on

being offended," said Mr Ali as he opened the door for Colin.

As he was riding back home, which was just on the edge of the village, the Council road sweeper, Donnie MacLean, affectionally known as, 'Donnie the Brush,' waved him down.
 "Hello Meenister, how are you and your good lady? Both keeping well, I hope." But before Colin could answer, Donnie said, "Were you hearing that a boatload of travellers landed at Culmore bay last night?"

"Yes, we are both well thank you Donnie. What's all this about travellers arriving in the night?" Colin asked.
"Aye, they landed without a sound, even old Mrs McColl who lives by the bay didn't hear a thing and she is said to hear the sun rising!"
"And who *are* these people?" Colin was intrigrued.
Donnie looked around to be sure that no-one was listening. "Nobody knows where they

come from or where they go – but they always appear on the night of the full moon.

We call them 'na feadhainn dorch' – the dark ones, for strange things happen when they are around." Donnie looked genuinely unsettled.

"What sort of strange things?" Colin asked.

"Dark and sinister things Meenister. The dogs howl and the cows fail to give milk. Aye and worse too, things that no Christian tongue would dare utter..."

"But you can tell *me* Donnie, I'm the Minister."

Donnie wasn't so sure but after some thought he looked around again and whispered dramatically, "Things no man can explain. The last time they visited the island, a lone white stag was seen seven times, even although there is no such beast on the Island – except in the stories of long ago which our forefathers have passed on to us.

One time, a few years ago, when the 'dark ones' came, Jock McLean went mad and jumped into the sea and swam out until he was out of sight, he was never seen again. Mind you, they found

a Whisky Still in his barn with a tin mug and a bucket of white spirit which was only half full."
Colin wasn't sure whether to smile or frown.

"And then there was the time that Mrs Mc Neill's cow gave birth to twin calves and never was she introduced to a bull – the cow that is."

"Oh dear, very strange goings on, as you say Donnie."
"Aye," said Donnie shaking his head.
"Well, thank you for warning me – will you let me know if anything else happens?"
"Aye, I will that. Strange things _will_ happen, you can be sure of that, Meenister."

Colin put his helmet back on and took off for home while Donnie carried on sweeping the roadside, looking left and right, as if watching for some 'other-worldly' being to confront him at any moment.
Back in the village, seven dark skinned and weather-beaten men skulked along the streets like hungry wolves in search of prey. The

villagers crossed over to the other side of the street, crossed themselves, spat on the ground and turned around three times as the strangers passed by.

"Don't look in their eyes mo nighean òg *(my young girl)*" a mother said to her young daughter and bustled her away.

 Just then the skies darkened and the rain and mist came down over the village, giving an air of foreboding.

As the men entered Mr Ali's shop, the ladies dropped their messages onto the floor and there was a mass exit through the store room and out of the back door.
Mr Ali's stomach was churning as he said, "I'm.. er, sorry gentlemen but the shop is … um…closed today."
The strangers stopped, slowly turned and stared at Mr Ali who was sure they were giving him the 'evil eye,' as the locals called it.

"But...of course..." Mr Ali stuttered, "If you er.. need anything I would be honoured to serve you. Please just choose what you want and bring it up to the counter, just when you are ready, there's no hurry now."

The shadowy men gathered bread and a few essential such as whisky and rum and left the shop without paying.

Mr Ali called after them, "Yes gentlemen, thank you, take them with my compliments." He was shaking and had to sit down for a few minutes to steady himself.

The ladies cautiously returned to the shop and listened to Mr Ali as he told them how he had bravely told them to get out of his shop and not to darken his door again.

"It's brave that you are Mr Ali," said one of the ladies.

Mr Ali bowed his head and with a modest smile said, "Och, it was nothing ladies, I wasn't going to let them get the better of me in my own shop!"

Just then, a loud clap of thunder crashed and a bolt of lightning flashed outside the shop. The ladies screamed and Mr Ali jumped behind the ample Mrs McVittie for safety.

"Oh mercy, there are dark forces at work right enough!" said Mrs McCrimmond, the Free Church Minister's wife.

Within minutes however, the sun was shining and it was as if the whole incident had never happened, except that Mr Ali and the ladies in the shop were left shaking in their boots.

Colin had almost made it home when the heavens opened and he got soaked.
'That's very strange' he thought, *'just a few minutes ago it was a lovely day, so much for the BBC Home Service forecast!'*
He put his motorbike in the shed and ran over to the back door. Lorna quickly opened the door and Colin hurried in.

"Come away in sweetheart. Look at you, you're soaked, away and get dried off or you'll catch your death of cold! I'll put the kettle on.

Oh, and the phone has been busy, you've to phone Mrs MacMaster back, she's in an awful state and asking for you. She said the 'dark ones' are here again. That means the whole island will be on edge. Strange things happen when *they* are around."

A few minutes later, Colin ambled in from the bathroom with a towel around his waist and drying his hair with another.

"Aye, so Donnie the Brush was telling me. They're probably a family of tinkers making their way over to Castlebay and on up to Harris, maybe for a tinkers wedding. Is it not just a load of superstitious nonsense anyway?"

"Oh mercy *no*, Colin! When we were young we were terrified of them, mother wouldn't let me out of the house when they were around. Our Teacher in the school told us they were descendants of an Irish Folklore figure called, 'Donn Fírinne', 'The Dark One', King of the Dead, and they speak in an ancient tongue that no one has spoken since time began. They say that the thunder and lightning means that Donn Fírinne is riding on his horse through the sky. Unusual and un-natural things _do_ happen I can tell you." Lorna looked genuinely anxious.

"Gosh, Lorna!" Colin said as he gave her a hug. "You're shaking, whatever's the matter? Surely you don't believe the silly nonsense about ancient mythological pagan kings and supernatural horses flying through the sky, do you?"

"It's not nonsense!" Lorna pulled away. "I've seen things Colin, things I don't ever want to see again, and I've heard so many stories that I _know_ it's not nonsense!"

Colin could see that Lorna was upset so he thought the best thing to do was to change the subject and make a cup of tea.

"Okay sweetheart, I believe you. Go and take a seat 'ben the house' and I'll get dressed and make us a nice cup tea – and I've got Custard Creams!" he said as he waved the packet of biscuits, bringing a smile to Lorna's bonnie face.

"Och, how can I resist you when you have the Custard Creams?"

As Colin was getting dressed the phone rang and Lorna answered. "He's just in the door this very minute Mrs MacMaster, wait you and I'll get him."

"Hello Mrs MacMaster and what can I do for you today?" Colin said cheerfully.

"It's the 'dark ones,' Meenister, they're prowling about our byre and sheds outside. Duncan won't go out and chase them and I don't blame him. I fear that the *droch fhortan* (bad luck) will be upon us, Meenister."

"Have you called the police? I'm sure PC Malcolm will help you, I'm not really in the strong-arm business Mrs MacMaster."

Mrs MacMaster nearly exploded, "Bookem!? He goes into hiding when they appear on the island!"

Colin smiled at the policeman's by-name of 'Bookem' derived from his propensity to book anyone who crossed his path.

"You will just have to come down yourself and give us a blessing, Meenister!" Mrs MacMaster was slowly working herself up into a state of extreme agitation. "You are a man of God, could you not put a curse on them?"

"I don't do curses Mrs MacMaster but I *will* come down to your croft and see if I can talk to them."

Lorna was listening and wasn't happy with the way the conversation was going.

When Colin had got off the phone she was distressed. "Oh Colin, don't be going out! Bad things happen when the 'dark ones' are around. Please, please stay safe here in the house, my love."

"But I can't sweetheart, Mrs MacMaster is up to high-doh, I'll have to go and see what's going on." Colin wasn't too keen on meeting the dark strangers either but knew it had to be done. *'We can't have the whole Island hiding in their homes, afraid to go out. It's time that someone stood up to them. I'm not afraid, I have a higher power watching over me,'* Colin thought to himself.

As he pulled up at the MacMaster's croft he understood how the young shepherd boy David must have felt when facing the Giant Goliath.

He took a deep breath, got out of the car and was met by Mrs MacMaster who took him around the back and pointed to the shed where she had seen the 'dark ones' prowling about.

"It's there that they are Meenister, round the back. I heard them speaking in their strange tongue. It's like nothing I have ever heard before, or want to hear again."

She could see that Colin wasn't too keen on rushing in. "Don't be worrying, the good Lord himself will be with you – and I'll be behind you with the poker!"

Colin steeled himself, said a wee prayer and walked down to the barn where he stopped and listened.

"Hello, is there anybody there?" He called.

'Oh goodness, he's summoning up supernatural help!' Mrs MacMaster thought.

He heard their guttural voices coming from behind the shed and he peered round to see the dark ones arguing over their haul of gold and silver chains and other items stolen from the good people of Rhua. They were a gruesome looking bunch, growling and snarling at each other.

Colin had come prepared, and took out a small brownie camera from his pocket and proceeded to take pictures of the gang counting their ill gotten gains. Now he had the proof he needed to implement his plan.

The voices grew louder and more aggressive until one of them pulled a knife out of his jacket and attacked one of his companions, sparking off a violent fight between them all.

One by one the travellers realised they were being watched.

One of the men had a severe gash down the side of his face and blood was flowing down over his neck and clothing.

"That's enough!" Colin shouted. "Throw down your knife!" At first they were surprised, but the man with the knife was bolder than his companions and stepped forward brandishing a long curved blade, shouting a stream of abuse in a language that Colin had never heard before, but he knew he wasn't saying, "Have a nice day Minister."

Then the man shouted in broken English, "A curse be upon you Meenister, and all your heirs through all the generations!" as he made a move towards Colin.

Just at that, a voice rang out from behind the strangers which made them turn around. "I wouldn't if I was you!" It was Mrs MacMaster wielding a very large iron poker!

At first the strangers laughed at the very thought of being threatened by an elderly lady with a poker, but then another voice rang out from behind Colin, causing the men to turn back round to face Colin again. It was Donnie wielding his trusty brush! "Don't you be hurting our Meenister! Or you'll have my brush to answer to!"

With Mrs MacMaster behind them and Colin and Donnie facing them, they were disorientated for just a moment as a booming voice from behind them shouted, "Drop the knife lads, the games up!" They turned back round to see PC John Malcolm, aka Bookem, facing them. He was a formidable sight, well over 6 feet 6 and an ex Ballachulish shinty player with a build to match, and he wasn't taking any nonsense.

The seven strangers could see that their adversaries meant business and weren't intimidated by their threats.

They were considering making a run for it when their companion who had been badly cut, fell down and seemed to be lifeless.

"Come on boys," Colin said, "give yourselves up, we need to help your friend. If you don't, one of you will be facing a murder charge, and I have the evidence right here," and he held the camera up for them to see.

They could see that it was all over, the knife was dropped and they held their hands up in the air. Bookem went forward and put handcuffs on two of the men (as he only had two sets of handcuffs) and tied the wrists of the other four men with bailing twine. Mrs MacMaster went indoors and called the District Nurse, a young Irish woman known as 'Maggie Nurse,' to deal with the injured man lying on the grass.

Maggie Nurse appeared within a few minutes and administered first aid on the wounded thug before putting him in the back of her little van and taking him down to the surgery, with Duncan MacMaster riding shotgun, just in case of any trouble.

"Aye, he's a brave man now that the tinkers are all in handcuffs!" said Mrs MacMaster.

Bookem was all set for booking the strangers but Colin called him aside and said that he had a plan and asked him to play along for now.

"Aye ok, it's devious that you are – for a Meenister!"

He winked at Colin and said in a stern voice, "Come on now boys, it's big trouble that you are in, it's the jail for you! By the time you see daylight again you'll be drawing the pension!"

They hung their heads as Bookem led them away.

Lorna arrived on her bike and called out to Colin, "Are you alright sweetheart!? Mrs MacMaster phoned to say what happened and you were so brave!" and she ran over and hugged him.

"He _is_ a hero Mrs Campbell, a _real_ hero!" said Donnie. "He faced them down until they gave up the ghost!"

"Och don't exaggerate Donnie, it was thon big brush you were wielding that gave them the fear!" Colin said with a smile.

"Aye, it's my Number one brush. The one I use for sweeping the snow off the roads in the winter," Donnie said proudly.

Later that day, Colin went down to see Bookem.
 "My plan should make sure that we never see them again on Rhua, will you trust me?" Colin asked.

"I'm not sure what you are up to Meenister but as it's yourself, I'll go along with your plan. But if it doesn't work, by chove I'll book the buggers!" and his eyes glazed over at the thought of booking seven people all at once, perhaps his ambition to be promoted to Sergeant might come sooner than expected!

 Word soon got round the island that the Minister had saved them from the 'dark ones' and he was hailed as a hero.

The stories of what actually happened became more exaggerated with each telling of it.

One version even had Colin fighting off all seven with a long knife, with his face covered in blood!

After two days of being held in the small island jail, early one morning, the 'dark ones' set off from Culmore Bay heading North East to

Castlebay, waved off by the Minister and PC Bookem.

"We're well rid of the blaggards!" said Bookem.

"Aye, we'll not see them on Rhua again, John."

"What did you say to them that made them so willing to leave Rhua and promise never to come back?" Bookem asked Colin, fascinated to hear how the Minister had managed to persuade them to leave.

"Only if you promise to keep this to yourself?"

"Of course, Meenister!" Bookem nodded.

"Well, I said that if they left and promised never to come back, I would make the photos of them with their ill gotten gains 'disappear' and you wouldn't arrest them, and no more would be said. But if they ever returned to Rhua, you would arrest them and I would give the Police the photo's for evidence! They would be put into Oban jail and Sergeant Galbraith would throw away the key!"

"Och it's fly that you are! And what about the Tinkers Curse, are you not worried about it?"

"Certainly not. He told me he would lift the curse, but I wasn't worried if he didn't because it's all a load of nonsense, my *higher* power has more authority than any Tinker's Curse."

"Aye Meenister, it's right that you are," said Bookem and they sat in silence for a few minutes as they took it all in.

"What a carry-on, eh?" Bookem said shaking his head, "You wouldn't get this sort of thing in Ballachulish!"

Colin laughed at Bookem's catch phrase.
"You're an awful man, John, so you are."

To everyone's relief, the 'dark ones' were never seen on Rhua again.

*

P.S.
Colin sent the photographic spool to the chemist in Oban to be developed, and after 2 weeks they came back on the Tuesday ferry.

He opened the envelope and handed the photos to Lorna.

"Wait till you see these Lorna, you'll see just what a desperate bunch we fought off!" He was beginning to believe the stories that were doing the rounds.

She looked at each photo in turn and had a puzzled expression on her face.
"What is it sweetheart?" Colin asked.
"Well, I'm not sure," she said and handed him the photos.
He looked at them, one by one, but all he could see was the back of the barn and a patch of bare grass, no jewellery, no 'dark ones,' only Mrs MacMaster looking at Colin with a fierce look on her face and brandishing a very large poker !

Mmmm, very strange, very strange indeed!

Chapter 3

The Minister and the Bothan...

Foreword : A Bothan is an illegal drinking hut, usually found in a remote area, which supplies cheap alcoholic drink and homemade spirits, also known as 'firewater, hooch or gut rot.'

*

The rain was coming down with a vengeance and the mist floated across the Machair as the Rev. Colin Campbell drove out to visit one of his flock, Mrs Gillies.

After church the previous Sunday he had been told that she was poorly and 'needing a wee visit from the Meenister.'

The Rev, as he was affectionately called by some, was happy to oblige as he enjoyed a good chat and a scone with home-made jam with his Parishioners. The tongue of good report had gone before her and Mrs Gillies's scones and home made Bramble jam were legendary on Rhua - and beyond.

Weather permitting, the Rev's favourite mode of transport was his motorbike, however, the frequent wet weather on the Isle of Rhua meant that the car was used more often than not.

As he drove across the open land, the visibility was slowly getting worse and Colin was surprised to see how busy the back road to Mrs Gillies's croft was. There were pushbikes, tractors and vans going this way and that.

As he rounded a particularly sharp bend he came across a tractor in a ditch with four men standing around discussing, in Gaelic, how best to get it back on the road.

As he slowed down he noticed that they were all soaked to the skin, but it didn't seem to bother them. Colin opened the passengers window and asked if there was anything he could do to help. "No, you're fine Meenister, it's very kind of you but we have everything under control," said a large, red faced character.

Colin smiled, "Okay boys, see and get out of the rain as soon as you can, you'll catch pneumonia if you're not careful."

"It's kind that you are Meenister, we will need to get something to warm us up, eh lads?" The boys laughed and Colin drove off. He looked in his rear-view mirror and saw the men laughing and passing round what looked like a bottle of lemonade. *"Lemonade won't keep them very warm on a day like this,"* he thought as he drove away up the road and on to Mrs Gillies's small croft and parked by the back door.

Mrs Gillies was a petite lady with a big smile. "Oh, come away in Meenister," she shouted from the doorway, "hurry or you'll get soaked." Colin sprinted from the car to the croft in record time and Mrs Gillies shut the door behind him. "It's no' half dreich Meenister, it's cats and dogs that it's raining! Let's be getting that jacket off you and I'll dry it by the fire."
Colin gladly obliged and before he knew it he was sitting by a roaring peat fire with a dram of whisky in one hand and a scone in the other.
"It's very kind of you Mrs Gillies, it certainly knows how to rain in Rhua doesn't it?"

"Aye, it does that Meenister, but at least it keeps the midgies at bay. Oh, and please call me Effie, it's short for Euphemia, after my dear grandmother." She smiled and poured out a dram for herself. "It keeps out the cold as my late husband used to say!" Colin took to Mrs Gillies straight away.

They spent over an hour chatting, more than he had intended, but she told him her life story, how her and her late husband had met and how they ended up on Rhua, it was a fascinating story.

Colin never ceased to be amazed at the life stories of those seemingly quiet and humble people he ministered to. From unsung war heroes' to the two sweet old ladies who had worked in the Forestry cutting down trees in their youth, and an elderly lady who had worked in Bletchley Park cracking codes during the second world war.
Mrs Gillies's story was no less unexpected. She had been an acrobat in a circus and had been

better known as, 'The 'Fying Flea' before meeting her husband in Glasgow and moving up to Rhua, her husband's family croft.

"I can still touch my toes," she said proudly.

"In fact, I'm sure I could still do a back flip if I tried." She stood up and was about to spring into action when Colin said, "Oh please be careful Mrs Gillies! Perhaps we should leave that for another day?"

"Okay Meenister, if you say so, and it's Effie, remember," she said, and sat down. Colin got the impression that she was glad to be stopped before she hurt herself.

The conversation was flowing and they both thoroughly enjoyed the visit.

"Well, Mrs..er.. Effie, I'd better be going, I still have to finish my notes for the Bible study group this evening. It's been lovely meeting you and I'm so glad to hear that you are on the mend. Will we be seeing you on Sunday?" Colin said as he stood up.

"Yes Meenister, if my back holds out," she said with a pained look on her face.

Oh, while I remember - here are my offerings for the past few Sundays." Then she jumped up, oblivious to her 'bad back,' and handed Colin a pile of coins which she had been keeping in a fruit bowl on the side-board.

Colin said a short prayer and left feeling happy and blessed to have such lovely people in his congregation.

As he drove back across the narrow road he came upon the same four lads still standing at the roadside. They were now laughing loudly and seemingly oblivious to the heavy rain. The water ran into the neck of their shirts, down their backs, through the legs of their dungarees and into their boots.

The tractor was still on its side in the ditch and the lemonade bottle was now empty and lying on the grass verge.

"Oh, here comes the Meenister!" one of the lads called out. "We'd better be on our best behaviour!" said another, much to the amusement of the 'boys.'

Before Colin had a chance to speak, an old bodach (gentleman) on a rusty bicycle came flying down the road and went straight into the ditch beside the group, his tweed cap flew up in the air and landed on the bonnet of Colin's car.

"Oh my goodness!" Colin said as he jumped out of the car to help the man out of the ditch.

"Don't you be worrying Meenister, old Duncan is no stranger to the ditches, he is in and out of them most days! We call him *Speedy*." said the red faced man.

"Why does he keep on crashing? His bike certainly looks like it's about to fall to bits at any minute!" Colin said.

"No Meenister, it's not the bike that causes the crashes," came the reply and the boys all looked at each other and laughed."

"Well, what *is it?*"

"It's the lemonade, Meenister!" one of the group said, which caused great hilarity among the waterlogged men.

They were soaked, inside and out.

Speedy and his bike were helped out of the ditch, he put on his cap with the peak facing backwards (for the greater aero-dyno-ism) and took off at great speed down the road, causing the lads to give a great cheer.

"Lemonade?" queried Colin.
"Och it was ..er.. just the joke we were having," said the most vocal of the group.
"Oh. right..." said Colin sceptically, feeling there was something he was missing.
"Well, this won't get the Fergie out of the ditch, eh boys?" one of the lads said, giving a nod and a wink.
"Oh..er..oh aye, of course. We'd better crack on Meenister."
Colin felt that was his cue to leave but he wasn't sure why or what was going on. "Ok lads, I'd better get home to the good lady, be sure and get yourself dried out soon."
"Aye Meenister it's the drying out that we need!" and they all laughed, including Colin, although he wasn't too sure just what he was laughing at.

The rain didn't let up all the way home and Colin had to make a run from the car into the Manse.

"What a dreich day," Colin said as he went through to the back scullery to take off his waterproof coat.

Lorna came thought to help him. "How was Mrs Gillies?"

"Oh, she was in good spirits but..."

"But what, sweetheart?"

"Just, well, something strange happened on the way home..." and he related the whole, 'tractor and lemonade' incident.

"I haven't been over the back road for a long time," Lorna said, "but I've heard rumours that it's a place for the heavy drinking."

"There was a big red faced fellow who seemed to have a good head of steam on him, I'd say."

"That'll be Angus John Mcaulay," Lorna said. "He's known for taking a good bucket. He can be a bit of a trouble maker when he takes too much."

"Oh dear, maybe I should have a word with PC Bookem, perhaps he can shed some light on the matter."

"Good idea sweetheart, he'll know what to do."

The next morning Colin called 'Bookem' and described his encounter with the 'boys' and Lorna's comments about it being a place for heavy drinking.

"Oh aye, I know Angus John alright!" Bookem told Colin. "He's an awful lad, a real trouble maker if ever there was. I've had my suspicions for some time that something is going on over there. Leave it with me Meenister and I'll get back to you when I know more."

It was to be PC Bookem's first real 'case' for a while and he was keen to find out just what was going on.

The next few weeks saw him making discreet enquiries and a number of undercover surveillances, which were cleverly carried out by riding his bike around the roads wearing his civilian clothes and his hat pulled down to cover his face.

Every now and then he would stop and update his notes in his Police issue notebook.

More often than not, some of the locals would pass by and either toot or wave at him, but he would look the other way and bury his head in his jacket. *'Aye, it's fly that I am! They'll never know me with my disguises,'* he said to himself.
In reality, of course, they all knew fine well who was skulking around the 'back' district of the Island – and why.

His most impressive piece of detective work was the all-night stakeout which really paid off and brought his investigation to a head. The only 'fly in the ointment' was about 2 a.m. one morning when he was hiding behind a rusty old tractor, and Mrs MacLean came out and offered him a dram and a marmalade sandwich, to keep out the cold.

"Oh Mr Bookem it's the death you will be catching, lying out in the damp grass at this hour!" she said kindly.

Later that day Bookem visited the Manse to update Colin on his progress.

"It's a sorry tale right enough Meenister," said Bookem shaking his head. "It's the drink that has got a hold of them, aye, it's the work of 'Donald Dhu' (*the devil*) himself!"

"What is? What have you uncovered?" Colin was anxious to find out what was going on.

"Is it a coven?" Colin asked, fearing some dark clandestine group, meeting on the machair at midnight.

"No, not a coven but a Bothan, Meenister, aye, a Bothan," said Bookem, shaking his head.

Coming from Glasgow and having been brought up in a fairly well to do family, Colin had no idea what a Bothan was, so he asked the obvious question, "What on earth is a Bothan?"

"Oh dear, Meenister, you have a lot to learn about the Islands. It's an illegal den of iniquity. Ochone, it's a sad day to be sure, when good God fearing people can't go about their business without being offered cheap drink which is only good for dipping the sheep!"

Bookem was genuinely upset.

"But I have the measure of them, by jove I'll put a spoke in their wheels! Are you up for putting a stop to their little games, Meenister?"

Colin wasn't so sure about that. "Well, what exactly do you have in mind?" he asked Bookem.

"We'll surprise them and catch them at their ungodly business. We'll have them!" Bookem could see his promotion getting ever closer. Sergeant Galbraith in Oban couldn't ignore him after this! *Man, it'll be the headlines in all the Papers, perhaps I'll even get a mention in the Oban times!* **'Police Constable foils unholy drinking den.'** I might even get a medal!" Bookem's imagination took flight.

"We'll go in at midnight!" he said firmly.

"But tomorrow is Sunday." Colin reminded him.

"Och, it's right that you are Meenister, we'll have to wait for Monday, we cannot be breaking the Sabbath. I'll come for you at a minute past midnight on the Monday morning and by golly we'll make short work of them!"

And that is how it was left.

On Sunday, Bookem fine tuned his plan of action while Colin preached on 1st Corinthians 6 : 10, "*Nor thieves, nor covetous, nor drunkards will inherit the kingdom of God.*"

That night, true to his word, Bookem pulled up outside the Manse at one minute after midnight. Colin crept out of the Manse, and with a strong sense of foreboding, he jumped into Bookem's police van. As they drove away Bookem laid out his plan to Colin.

"I've seen them coming and going at all hours, day and night, singing and carrying on – aye and on the Sabbath day too! So here's the plan. I have found a clump of bushes behind Alec Morrison's old tractor, where we can get sight of the Bothan. You can't see it from the road but there's a path coming up from the Machair. We'll wait until the time is just right and then we'll pounce!"

Colin had never 'pounced' on anyone before, but he couldn't back out now, and besides that, it was all for the good of the moral and spiritual welfare of the community.

They got themselves in position and settled down, observing a good number of men coming and going in and out of the wee wooden hut.

Bookem had been right – and there was singing too!

After about an hour or so, a good crowd had entered the Bothan and Bookem felt it was time to strike.

"Ok Meenister, let's go, and may the good Lord go with us!" and he stood up and beckoned Colin to follow on.

The pair crept stealthily towards the hut, when all of a sudden, all went quiet. Colin and Bookem looked at each other, 'what was going on?'

Just as they decided to storm the hut, the singing started up once more. Bookem nodded to Colin as he stepped forward and gave the wooden door a mighty kick with his size 13 Police issue boot, and they both rushed in.

"Nobody move!" Bookem shouted.

What confronted them was beyond anything they could have ever imagined.

Approximately 20 men were sitting in a circle, Bibles in hand, singing the 23rd Psalm, in the Gaidhlig!

Bookem and Colin stood there, speechless and confused.
"Oh, it's yourself PC Malcolm – and the Meenister too, what a lovely surprise, come away in we're just about to put up a prayer," said one of the group.
"But... but... I thought..." Bookem was lost for words. Colin was completely dumfounded too.

"It's God's good providence that he brought you here tonight. We're having a wee service of thanksgiving, thanking the good Lord for having such a fine Po-lis constable as yourself, and a first rate Meenister as Reverend Campbell, to keep us poor sinners safe in body and in soul. Glory be!" to which all the 'congregation' replied, "Glory be!"
It was the red faced character that Colin had encountered drinking the 'lemonade' a few days earlier, Angus John Macauley.

It took a few moments for Bookem to regain his composure.

"You're up to something! Only the good Lord knows what exactly, but you can be sure I'm going to find out!"

"It's blessed that we are, right enough, to have such a dedicated Polis-man as yourself." Angus John declared with a smile.

Bookem herumphed as he looked behind empty boxes and in every corner, but could find nothing incriminating.

"Come away Meenister, we'd better be going – but we'll be back! Mark my words, we'll be back!"

"But we're just away to sing a psalm, can you not stay on?" Angus John said in all seriousness. Bookem stormed out of the little wooden hut with Colin following on behind.

As they made their way back to the police van, they could hear much laughter coming from the hut. Bookem was furious, "I'll get the beesoms, be sure of that, I'll get them!"

Colin wondered how the locals managed to clear away the drink and be sitting like angelic cherubs when he and Bookem had burst in.

Little did he know that his clandestine surveillance outings had been observed, and the raid was expected, and so a plan had been hatched. Colin couldn't help but smile at their resourcefulness.

Thereafter, even up to this very day, the Bothan on the wee Island of Rhua is still known as, 'The Holy Bothan.'

*

Foot notes :

<u>Machair</u> : a fertile low lying grassy plain. This is the Gaelic name given to one of the rarest habitats in Europe which only occurs on exposed Western coasts of Scotland and Ireland.

* <u>Beesom</u> : (1) a broom made of twigs similar to those we usually associate with witches.

(2) It is also a term of contempt for a difficult person, as in - "Ya wee beesom!"

Chapter 4

The Minister and the Black Book of Rhua...

Foreword : 'The Black Book of Rhua' is a book of poems, spells and mysterious tales. It was thought to have the power against curses, spells and fairy enchantments. The original handwritten book has been lost for centuries. This Tale is loosely based on the legend of the ancient, 'Red Book of Appin.'

*

It was a rainy day as Reverend Colin Campbell drove home after conducting the funeral service of a well known and well respected resident of Rhua, Mr Johnson, who had lived on the island for over 20 years but was still considered an incomer by the older members of the community.

He was a quiet, kindly man who had been a Professor of Classics at Oxford University. He had opted out of the rat-race and moved to Rhua after his wife passed away. She was of West

Highland stock and longed to return to Scotland, but the busyness of academic life had kept them in Oxford until her sad passing 23 years ago. He never forgave himself for not moving back to Scotland sooner and was a melancholy figure, often seen wandering along the shores and roads of the Island.

"How did the funeral go sweetheart?" Lorna asked Colin as he came in and sat down at the kitchen table.

"It went well, I think. There was a great turn out, the church was packed."

"Aye, I'm not surprised," replied Lorna. "He was a lovely man, always polite when he met you in the village, such a shame."

The weeks following the funeral saw Colin kept busy with the usual Ministerial duties such as, planning next Sunday's service, visiting his parishioners. writing his sermon, visiting couples regarding the Baptism of their child, school assemblies and all the other, unexpected things, which crop up each week.

However, one morning the Manse phone rang, and a voice said, "Hello is that the Meenister?"

"It is," Colin answered, "And who am I talking to?"

"It is myself," came the reply.

Colin smiled and said, "And what can I do for *yourself*?"

"Well, I am the cousin of the late Mrs Johnson, the wife of the late Professor Johnson, do you remember, you conducted his funeral a few weeks ago? And it was an uplifting service if I may say so."

"Oh yes, thank you. Dear Mr Johnson, such a lovely man," Colin replied.

"Well, my good lady and myself went over to clear out his croft, and we found a couple of boxes of old books which we thought you might like to have, seeing as you're the Meenister."

"Well, that's very kind of you but…"

"Great! I'll come up by the Manse and drop them in this afternoon," and the phone went dead.

"Who was that sweetheart?" Lorna could see that Colin was perplexed.

"I'm not quite sure… but… whoever he is, he's coming to the Manse this afternoon with a couple of boxes of books."

"Oh no! Not more books! Is the house not full of books already!?"

"Yes, I tried to tell him that but he hung up before I could say anything," Colin said in self defence.

"Oh well, we will just have to wait and see." Lorna was slightly irritated and felt quite sure that Colin would never say 'no' to more books.

Later that day a rusty old van appeared at the Manse and two men carried 4 boxes and a sack up to the front door.

"Oh my goodness," Colin said as he looked out of the window, hoping that Lorna wasn't looking too.

By the time he had opened the front door, there were at least 6 boxes piled by the door.

"Goodness me! I thought you said there were 'a couple' of boxes."

"Aye that's right Meenister - and there is a couple more, too."

All in all, there were 10 boxes and two sacks full of books.

Just as Colin was counting them, Lorna appeared at the door. "Mercy me! Whatever is all this?"

"Books missus, the Meenister said to bring them round."

Lorna gave Colin a glower.

"It wasn't my idea! I thought there was just one or two boxes." Colin explained.

But Lorna wasn't convinced and before she could say anymore, the men jumped into their van and drove off.

"We can put them in the back scullery, they'll be out of the way for now," Colin offered.

"Put them where you like, just so long as they aren't under my feet!" Lorna was not best pleased.

Fifteen minutes later Colin had carried all the boxes, and the sacks of books through the house and out into the back scullery and covered them with a blanket.

'*It's going to take me quite a while to sort through all these!*' Colin thought to himself as he picked up a box, carried it into his study, closed the door and stayed in there until the atmosphere in the house became a bit warmer.

Between work and reading through the books, it took a few weeks to go through all the boxes. He put those of interest to one side and re-boxed the others for future disposal.
They were a fascinating assortment of books from Classical Greek Mythology, various religious and theological books plus a variety of spiritual and mystical books, manuscripts and articles from around the world.

He had kept the 2 sacks to last and it was here that he found the most interesting books and a number of faded manuscripts in manila folders.

There were dusty old Bibles in Greek, Latin and Aramaic, with the Creation Story, *found in the book of Genesis*, hand written in a language that Colin didn't recognise. Was it the legendary

'Adamic' language which is said to be the language that Adam and Eve used to communicate with God and He with them? If so, then this was an academic treasure to be sure.

Colin had studied Early Greek, Ancient Hebrew, and some rudimentary Aramaic as part of his Divinity studies but he had never seen anything quite like this - it sent an exciting shiver down his spine.

He was about to delve into the fascinating text when Lorna called, "Here's a visitor to see you, Colin. Will you come through while I put on the kettle?"

"Ok sweetheart," he replied and went through to the front room where he saw a small, dark haired, sallow faced man.

"Good morning your Reverence," the visitor said as he removed his hat, "I am so sorry to intrude on your precious time Minister, my name is Doctor Alasdair McQueen, and I am carrying out research into the local superstitions and folklore in and around the Western Highlands and Islands.

I thought I should drop in and pay my respects to you, you being the Parish Minister."

"Well, that's very kind of you Doctor McQueen."

"Please, call me Alasdair," the visitor said with a forced smile.

"Oh, yes of course," Colin continued. "But I'm afraid that superstitions and the like are outwith my jurisdiction, Alasdair."

Dr McQueen pressed on – "I believe that you have recently been given all Professor Johnson's books and manuscripts, and I wondered if I might have a look through them for something which might help me in my research?"

Colin got the feeling that Dr McQueen (if indeed he *was* a Doctor) wasn't being totally honest with him. What was he up to?

"What is it you *really* want Dr McQueen?"

Seeing that he was not getting the information he was looking for, the stranger decided to be more direct.

"Well, I'll be honest with you Reverend, you being a man of the cloth.

I have spent many years tracking down some very rare religious manuscripts, and a couple of years ago my detective work led me to Oxford University, to Professor Johnson to be precise.

Two years or so after his wife passed away he seemed to disappear off the face of the earth, but I finally tracked him down to this God forsaken island."

Colin bristled at the insulting description of the beautiful island of Rhua.

"After talking to one or two local families," Dr McQueen continued, "I understand that there are a few 'interesting' books and manuscripts in the boxes you were given by his late wife's family. In particular, a small black book. It's of no real importance or significance but I would be interested to see it."

Colin's suspicions were aroused even further.

The visitor continued, "The family don't realise it but some of the books could be worth quite a bit and perhaps you and I could…well… make a pretty penny ourselves. What do you say?" He winked at Colin.

So that was it! He wasn't interested in the books for their academic importance but for how much he could make from them.

Lorna walked into the room with a tray of tea and biscuits and was just about to lay them on the table when Colin said, "Oh, we won't be needing those thank you darling, Dr McQueen is just leaving."

Lorna looked at Colin, "But, but… "

"I'll explain later sweetheart. Goodbye Dr McQueen, I don't think we have anything more to discuss." Colin opened the door and stood, waiting for his visitor to leave.

The stranger was not best pleased. "I'm sorry you are taking this attitude Reverend, you and I could have made quite a fortune if you have the manuscripts that I think you have."

"Well, as the good book says – 'No-one can serve two masters, you cannot serve both God and money,' Colin quoted from the Gospel of Matthew.

Dr McQueen gave a snort of contempt and strode indignantly out of the Manse.

"What on earth was that all about?" Lorna asked Colin as he closed the door firmly.

"I'm not quite sure, but I think that our Dr McQueen, if that *is* his name, is up to no good."

He told Lorna all that was said.

Lorna was quite shocked, "What a horrible little man! Mind you, I had my doubts. As my dear grandmother used to say, *"I don't like the look of him, his eyes are too close together!"*

Colin smiled and said, "Your grandmother sounds like a very wise lady. Perhaps we should put these valuable books and papers somewhere very safe! Aren't you pleased now that they brought us so many books?"

"Och, you…" Lorna laughed and gave Colin a hug.

Colin walked over to the front door and turned the key.

"Is that really necessary?" Lorna wondered if Colin wasn't being a wee bit over cautious.

"Well, you never know, there's been talk of a suspicious looking character going around the Island, and I think we've just met him. Better to be safe than sorry."

After lunch, Colin went to his study and looked through the 2 sacks of books and folders which he had set aside for future scrutiny.

There were a number of half written dissertations and some others that were in a language with which he wasn't familiar.

As he took out the various books and papers, a black, hand-bound book fell on to the floor. Colin glanced at it and his heart skipped a beat. *'Oh my goodness'* he thought to himself, *'It can't be, can it?'*

The pages were faded and it was hand written in what he guessed, from what little knowledge he had picked up, was an ancient form of Gaelic. Lorna had been teaching him to speak and read the Gaelic, a language which is still very much the first language of so many in the Western Islands and Highlands of Scotland.

He carefully opened the fragile pages and was able to pick out the odd word, but this was very different from anything he had come across before.

He called Lorna through to see if she could understand any of it but all she could say was, "This is very old Colin, there are very few around today that would know this old tongue. Perhaps old Mr McLean at CulBaithen Farm might be able to make some sense of it, he's very knowledgeable about the old ways."

The next morning, they visited Mr McLean over on the East side of the island.

Colin showed him a few of the books and papers he had been given.

"My goodness Meenister, it's quite the treasure trove you have here, to be sure," said the old crofter as his eyes scanned across the various texts. "Some of these are very old, very old indeed."

"What about this one Mr McLean?" Colin asked as he handed him the small, fragile, black book.

The moment he took the book in his frail hands, his eyes closed and he seemed to go into a dream-like state.

He whispered the words, "She has come home," in an old Gaelic tongue that Lorna could barely understand.

He stroked the pages gently, held them to his forehead and began to sob but no tears came.

Colin looked at Lorna with a, *'what should we do now?'* kind of look.

Just then Mr McLean's eyes opened wide and he asked, "Where in the name of all that is holy did you get this?"

Colin thought it best not to say too much but simply replied, "It recently came into my possession."

"Yes," said Lorna, "and we thought you were the very man to come to for help and advice."

"What you have here is the oldest, most revered book of our early ancestors, said to be written in a Gaelic-Norse language by Finn McCoull, the

Irish warrior chief and father of Ossian the Celtic Bard.

Ossian followed his father and wrote many poems telling of those early times, some of which were later added to this book.

He travelled around the Highlands and Islands by foot and by boat and collected stories, poems and mystical spells, many of which were gathered from the ancients here in Rhua where it is said that Ossian lived for a number of years.

It is known as, 'The Black Book of Rhua' and was written a long time ago when the veil between the worlds was thinner than it is today.

It was thought to have been lost forever when Ossian was attacked in a cave high on the hills above Glencoe in his later years, and many of his epic works were stolen.

There are verses that can call up a storm, and poems to calm them. Poems to heal the sick, bring a famine or invoke a rich harvest.

Much blood has been spilled trying to possess it.

A copy was found in the possession of a holy man who lived in Appin. It was thought to be the original but was later denounced as a fake.

But this…" Mr McLean held the book between his hands as if in prayer - "This, is the original, I'm sure of it. I can feel its vibrations running through my blood and its power surging through me.

Thanks be to the great God of time and space, of earth, wind and fire, of life and death, it has come home to guide his people, his family."

The tears of joy ran down his face as he uttered a blessing in an ancient Gaelic tongue that Lorna had not heard before but somehow understood. He handed the black book to Lorna who immediately felt a tingle move up her arms like a mild electric shock.

"I can feel it! I can hear the words being spoken. It's strange, although I can't understand the words on the page, I know what they are saying! How is that even possible?"

"Then you are truly blessed my dear," said Mr McLean. "The ancient words are only made clear to Seers and people of Finn Coull's direct descent and those who have the gift."

Lorna looked over to Colin in amazement, she was lost for words.

"Oh yes, the Mac Domhnall's or MacDonalds, as we now know them, are descended from Somerled who was a Norse-Gaelic Lord and became the Lord of Argyll and the Isles, which of course include Coll, Tiree and our own wee Island of Rhua," Mr McLean explained.

Lorna felt butterflies swirling around in her stomach. "My Grandfather once told me that our family, the MacDonald's, are related to Somerled and the Domhnall's but I thought it was just a tale he liked to tell the children.

And if I remember correctly, he also said that no-one in our family line had ever moved far away from the Islands, except the men who went off to the two great wars, but sadly very few of them returned home to their families and their crofts."

Mr McLean seemed to get more excited at this news. "That means that it is very likely that you are in the direct line of descendancy from the early Kings of Dalriada, the Lords of the Isles and the Norse-Gaelic line! Which makes you a very special lady indeed!"

Lorna didn't know what to say and just sat there staring into space as she tried to take it all in.
Colin smiled and said, "See, I told you that you were *special*, didn't I sweetheart!?"

Lorna felt overwhelmed with it all and her tears fell down her cheeks like a mountain burn.
Colin leaned over and held her hand as she wept.

After a few minutes, Colin asked Mr McLean, "So, what happens now?"
"Well, the first thing we *don't* do is make this public. There are lots of unscrupulous people out there who would love to get their hands on this wee book, so the fewer people who know about it the better, for now anyway."
"Funny you should say that," Colin said. "I had someone calling himself Dr McQueen asking

about it. I doubt that is his real name, or even if he is a genuine Doctor."

"Then we must be careful," said Mr McLean.
"The next thing is to get it authenticated by a respected body, then we can see where it takes us from there. I have an old friend who was a Professor in Aberdeen University who will help us. We studied the Norse-Gaelic texts and culture together many years ago. I can get in touch with him, if that is okay with yourselves? It might mean a trip over to Aberdeen, how would you feel about that?"

"What do you think sweetheart?" Lorna asked Colin.
"Well, I'm quite happy to follow Mr McLean's good advice, if you are?"
Lorna agreed that it sounded like the best way forward.
"Okay then," said Mr McLean. "I will get the ball rolling but meantime we must keep this between the three of us, tell absolutely *no-one*, is that agreed?"

Colin and Lorna nodded in agreement.

"Oh, and another thing," Mr McLean added, "You must keep it somewhere safe, we don't want to get this far and lose it to some unscrupulous thief!"

Colin and Lorna left Mr McLean's croft around lunch time with the book wrapped up in brown paper and tied up with string, concealed under Lorna's jacket – completely unaware that they were being watched.
They hurried back to the Manse, closed the door and locked it securely behind them.

"Well, I think this calls for a custard cream, what do you say sweetheart?"
"Aye," said Lorna, "and maybe a wee glass of sherry too!"
"A good idea - I'll get the sherry bottle if you get out the biscuits, we have a lot to think about." Colin said excitedly.

They sat sipping their sherry and nibbling their custard creams as they talked. *(Colin liked to nibble around the edges of the biscuit before biting into the creamy centre)*.

As they reflected on all that Mr McLean had said that morning. Lorna was finding it all too much to take in.

"Me, a direct descendant of Finn McCoull and Ossian? It's just too fantastic to believe. What do you make of it all, Colin?"

"Well, you're right sweetheart, it *is* a lot to take on board, but Mr McLean seems to know what he's talking about – and you have to admit that you *do* have an ability to 'see things' that not everyone else can, do you remember that time we were at the fairy well?"

Lorna smiled, "Well yes, I suppose that's true, but I've been able to see and speak to the Sidhe *(Shee/fairy)* folk since I was a wee girl, I thought it was normal."

"Well, it's *not* normal darling, very few people have the gift to 'see beyond,' Colin replied.

Lorna continued, "My grannie used to say that I had the 'second sight' when I told her of my strange dreams. Perhaps I am just a bit odd."
"Not odd but *special,* sweetheart," added Colin.

He rose and gave her a hug. "You will always be special to me." They held each other for a few moments and then Colin said, "I think we had better find a safe place to keep that wee black book, just in case. Any ideas?"
The afternoon was spent seeking out a good hiding place for the precious book.
From under the bed to under the kitchen sink. Many places were considered but eventually it was agreed that the last place an intruder would look was in a small metal box hidden under the pile of peats in the scullery.

"He'll never look for it there," Lorna said, "Just make sure you don't throw it on the fire by mistake!"

"Don't even joke about it!" Colin answered with a smile.

"I was thinking that we ought to tell father, after all he is a MacDonald too." Lorna said.

"Aye, maybe you're right," Colin agreed. "Perhaps we should go round later and tell him, and your mother too."

That evening they visited Lorna's parents' and explained all that had happened and what Mr McLean had said.

"Mercy me, who would have thought it?" Lorna's father said. "I know that most of my family haven't strayed far from the Islands. Why would they want to leave? Everything we could ever want, or need, is right here."

At one time Colin would have questioned the idea that everything they could ever want or need is right here on this remote island, but now he found himself agreeing with Harrold.

"Be careful you two, we don't want you getting in harm's way!" Lorna's mother added.

They spent the evening talking about it all, including their impending trip to Aberdeen."

Lorna mentioned that she would have to provide her birth certificate and various other family papers.
"Is there not a box or something under the bed, with all sorts of family photos and certificates? I remember seeing it when I was young, just after grannie had passed on – or am I havering?" Lorna asked.

"Aye, it's a suitcase, with all our birth certificates and goodness knows what else, your father will get it out and we can go through it and see what we can find."

*

Mr McLean didn't possess a telephone so any correspondence with his old University colleagues in Aberdeen was conducted by letter. Consequently, it was a few weeks before Colin and Lorna heard anymore from him.

Each day, and night, was interrupted by visits to the woodpile in the scullery to check that the treasured black book was still there.

One night, a week or so after visiting Mr McLean, Lorna had been wakened by something, or someone, outside.

She shook Colin's arm and whispered, "Colin, Colin, there's someone outside."
Sleepily, Colin answered – "It'll be the cat, go back to sleep sweetheart."
A few minutes later, Lorna shook his arm again and said "Colin, Colin."
"Yes, what is it now?"

"We don't have a cat!"

"Oh right," Colin answered as he stirred himself. He slowly pulled back the curtain and was sure he saw the shadow of a man creeping around.
"Yes, there's definitely someone lurking about outside." Colin closed the curtain quickly.

"I'll go and get the torch," Lorna said as she went through to the kitchen.

As she came back into the bedroom, Colin noticed that she had also picked up the rolling pin.

"Maybe they're after the book!?" Lorna said, her voice was shaking.

"Aye, that will be it! It's probably that Dr McQueen or whatever his real name is, he looked a desperate character, right enough."

Suddenly, there was a loud crash outside, followed by the 'ding' of a small bell - they knew that someone had just tripped over Lorna's pushbike which was leaning against the wall by the back door.

Lorna jumped and shouted, "Oh, God save us!"

"Okay sweetheart, stay calm," Colin whispered, but Lorna could see he was trembling too.

"We'll have to go out and see who it is!" Lorna was feeling a bit more courageous now and ready to go out and challenge the intruder.

"Don't be hasty now," Colin was hoping that the night-time visitor might just go away of his own accord.

"Come on, you take the torch and I'll take the rolling pin, just in case," said Lorna.

The two of them crept out of the front door and round to the back. As they stood, peering to see who it was, a large shadow loomed over them. "Quick! Shine the torch in his eyes, Colin, and I'll hit him over the head!"

Colin shone the light into the intruder's face and Lorna struck him over the head. It was all over in an instant.

Then there was silence.

It took a moment to sink in, but when they saw who it was, Lorna shouted, "God preserve us!"

It was PC Bookem!

He was lying on the ground rubbing his head. "What the...? I could arrest you for striking a Polis-officer in the doing of his duty!"

"Oh, Mr Malcolm, I am *so* sorry, we thought you were a thief, coming to rob us.

Oh dear, Colin, what have we done?"

"Let's get him inside and we can see how badly he is injured - maybe a wee dram will help."

They helped him into the kitchen and sat him down. "It's not so bad as it looks." Lorna said as she wiped his head with a damp cloth. "Just a wee scratch."

"A wee scratch!?" Bookem was not happy. "I've a good mind to arrest you both for gregarious bodily harm! You'd never get this kind of thing in Ballachulish!"

Two drams and one cup of tea later PC Bookem was feeling much better.

"What were you thinking, prowling around at night"? Lorna asked him.

"It was Mr MacDonald, your father, who put me up to it," Bookem said. "He was concerned that the two of you were in some kind of danger and asked me to keep an eye out, just to keep you safe."

Lorna was not best pleased, "Wait till I see him in the morning!"

Colin could see that she was upset. "He meant well sweetpea, he was just trying to watch out for us, to keep us safe, just as John said."

"Well, I'd better be going, who knows what's going on out there? Crimes could be in progress as I am sitting here, passing the time with yourselves?"

As he left the Manse, Bookem said quietly, "It might be a good idea if we were not to mention this incident, just incase it gets back to Sergeant Galbraith in Oban – he might push me into making a charge of Police brutality."

Colin and Lorna looked at each other and smiled. "Is that not when the Police attack a member of the public?" Lorna asked.

"Aye, just that," Bookem replied and left the house rubbing his head.

A few days later, early in the morning, there

came a knock on the door of the Manse. It was Mr McLean carrying an army canvass gas mask bag over his shoulder.

"Oh, it's yourself Mr McLean, come away in," Lorna said. "Colin, it's Mr McLean!" she shouted through the house.

"I hope I'm not being a bother Lorna, but I have some information that I thought you would like to hear."

"Goodness me, you are no bother, it's good to see you. Come through and have a seat and I'll put the kettle on."

Colin appeared and both he and Lorna sat in anticipation of the news that Mr McLean was about to impart.

"It's regarding the black book you brought to me a few weeks ago," Mr McLean said. There is good news and some not so good news."

"The good news is, that from my description, an old colleague of mine in the Gaelic Cultural Department of Aberdeen University, seems to think it might well be the real thing."

"And the 'not so good news'?" Lorna asked.

"As we thought, you will have to take it to Aberdeen University in person so that it can be authenticated, and you will also have to take your birth certificate and other family documents with you, for verification.

Perhaps you should plan a trip to Aberdeen for, say, 4 or 5 week's time. I will find out just exactly what paperwork they will be looking for and that will give you time to gather all you need to take with you.

Lorna was both shocked and excited. "Aberdeen! How far away is that?" Lorna had never been further than Oban in her life.

"Don't worry sweetheart, I know where it is. Let's just say that it's a long way away. Hopefully, we won't get lost!" Colin joked.

"Oh, my goodness, don't be saying that!" Lorna didn't know whether to laugh or cry.

"You will have to be on guard day and night," Mr McLean said. "There are lots of unscrupulous people out there who would love to get their hands on this book.

What about the stranger who came to see you, have you seen him again?"

"Yes, he's still around, I saw him in the village the other day, he looks a shifty character if ever there was one. We'll have to be very careful," replied Colin.

Mr McLean smiled and agreed, "You are quite right Meenister, that's why I think you should call in extra security – how about asking PC Malcolm to accompany you, to provide the 'muscle' should it be needed!"

"A good idea Mr McLean, with a big hefty Policeman like Bookem guarding it, it would take a pretty reckless character to try his luck. One glower from him would send even the most desperate criminal running a mile!" Colin answered with a smile.

"And don't forget," he continued, "I'll be on hand too, you know, in case there is any rough stuff."

Lorna wasn't sure if that was particularly comforting or not, but smiled anyway and said

"Of course, sweetheart," with less conviction than Colin would have liked.

"The University will cover your expenses," said Mr McLean. "This discovery has them in a whirl. It would be a real feather in their cap if they were the ones to break the news of its existence to the world."

He felt a tremor of excitement run up his spine at the very thought of it all.

As it turned out, PC Bookem wasn't given permission by Sergeant Galbraith to leave his post, in case a crime wave should hit the island in his absence.

So, after much preparation and planning, Colin and Lorna found themselves travelling to the far North East of Scotland.

Aberdeen, here we come!

It was a long, tense and tiring journey. From Rhua to Oban on the ferry, then a bus to Glasgow and a train up to Aberdeen – and all the while, the 'Black book' was secreted at the bottom of Lorna's handbag and every stranger who gave them more than a fleeting glance was seen as a potential book thief.

As they left the train at Aberdeen railway station, they were confronted by a taxi driver saying, "Fit like? Faar ye off till?" in a strong Doric accent.

Lorna and Colin looked at each other, wondering what strange language the man was speaking.

Since the end of the war there were many strangers in the country, not that they ever saw them in Rhua, except for Mr Ali in the shop and he spoke better Gaelic than some of the locals.

"I'm sorry," Colin said politely, "I didn't quite catch that."

"Ahh, I see, ye dinna come fae hereaboots then?" The taxi driver replied.

"Yes indeed," Colin replied, thinking he had finally got a grip on the lingo.

The driver realized that there was a definite language barrier and said very slowly, "Faar.. are.. ye.. off to?"

"Oh, where are we going to? Yes, the University please."

'At last,' the driver thought to himself, *'maybe now we can get going!'*

He loaded up the suitcases, said, "Pile in folks!" and before they knew it, they were heading along Union Street, down King Street to the entrance of the stately Aberdeen University.

Rather than attempt another conversation with the taxi driver, Colin held out a handful of coins and let the driver take his fare.

"One and thruppence," said the driver as he slowly counted out two sixpences and a thruppenny bit.

Lorna was feeling lost and completely out of her comfort zone. She had been to Oban a couple of times but never this far from the safety of her home in Rhua.

Colin was less concerned, after all, he had been born and brought up in the bustle of Glasgow – also known as, 'the dear green place.'

As they stood looking around, wondering which way to go, a young student walked by and asked, in a soft voice, if they needed any assistance.

"That would be good, thank you," said Colin. "We're looking for the Department of Gaelic and Scottish studies."

"It's not far from here, I'll walk round with you, follow me." said the student.

Lorna thought she detected a highland lilt in the young girl's voice. "Where is it you are from?" asked Lorna.

"Och, you'll not have heard of it, it's away in the islands. A wee place called Colonsay. I'm studying English literature; this is my final year. I want to be a teacher."

Lorna brightened up. "Colonsay! I have an aunt who lives there, Chrissie Cochrane, she's married on to Alastair the gamekeeper, they live up at Kiloran Bay. I'm from Rhua myself."

"Chrissie Cochrane!? She lives just across the bay from us!" said the young student.

Colin stood listening to them chatting, and it wasn't long before they slipped into the Gaelic. *'What are the chances of that?'* he thought, *'I wouldn't be at all surprised if they found out they were related!'*

"Aye, there's a few of us from the islands here. The other students call us the 'Gaelic mafia!' on account of they don't know what we're saying, but that suits us fine, especially when we're talking about the boys!" Lorna laughed. She felt so much better now.

Colin shook his head and smiled, he was quite sure that God had brought that young student from Colonsay into their path that day to bring comfort and assurance to Lorna.

He remembered the words in Isaiah Chapter 41:10, *'Do not be afraid for I am with you,'* and smiled. He was quite sure that God really *was* with them on their trip so far from home.

The next few days consisted of forensic tests on the book, as well as an examination of all Lorna's personal and family documents.

On day four, Lorna and Colin were called into a meeting with the Head of the Faculty and other leading professors and scholars who specialised in ancient and early Gaelic and Scottish culture.

Much of it went over Lorna and Colin's head. "What are they saying?" Lorna asked Colin, "Do they think it's genuine? Do they think *I* am genuine!? Oh mercy, the embarrassment if it all turns out to be a hoax!" Lorna was becoming anxious.

"Don't worry yourself sweetheart, from what I can gather from their discussions, all their tests and checks lead them to be 99.9 percent sure that the book is quite genuine. And there is no doubt in their minds that you *are* of the blood line of McDonald of MacDonald, Lord of the Isles," Colin explained.

"Oh Colin, it all seems too amazing to be true!" Lorna was struggling to take it all in.

"So, can I ask, what happens now?" she asked the group of academics who were excitedly talking among themselves.

"Well," one of the professors replied, "that is really up to you. We still have a couple of routine tests to complete but as you are the rightful heir to this historic book, it is up to you what you want to do with it."

"Gosh, I don't know, what are the options?"

"Well, in a nutshell, you can take it home or leave it here. But I must warn you that if word should get out that the book is with you on Rhua, there is the possibility of it being stolen, which will bring with it, the very real danger of harm coming to the two of you."

"Oh my goodness, what do you think?" Lorna said to Colin.

"Well, perhaps it would be better to leave it here. At least it will be safe, and so will we! But it's your decision sweetheart."

One of the other professors spoke up, "If I may say, you can be absolutely sure that we will keep it here under lock and key, in a secured cabinet in the exhibition room, where the public can see and enjoy it too.

It will still belong to you, and you can ask for it back at any time. It is also our practice to pay an annual sum for the loan of the book, and seeing as it is such a rare and historic book, that sum will be more than generous, after all, it will be a real feather in our cap, Celtic scholars will come from all over the world to see it."

"Well, I'd say that would be the best option. What do you think?" Colin said.

"Yes, I think you are right," Lorna agreed.

Turning to the group of experts, she said, "Yes, I would like to leave the book in your hands, for the safety of the book and of Colin and my family."

And so it was agreed.

Before leaving, Lorna had to sign a few legal documents and was handed a more than generous cheque in payment for the first year's loan of the ancient and unique book.

The Academics were overjoyed to have the book in their keeping – and Colin and Lorna were just pleased that it was all over and they could now get back to some peace and quiet on their lovely wee Island of Rhua.

Colin looked at the cheque, smiled and said, "Mmm, I could get myself a brand new motorbike with that!"

"Not so fast Geoff Duke," Lorna said. "I've got other plans for the money – like a new three piece suite for the living room!"

"Well, we'll see who gets their own way sweetheart," Colin said with an air of self-satisfaction.

"I think we already know the answer to that!" Lorna answered confidently.

The professor smiled and said to Colin, "Looks like it's going to be a new suite then?"

"Aye, looks like it." Colin smiled and gave Lorna a hug.

The next morning, they made the long journey back to the safety of the beautiful Island of Rhua, very much happier than when they had left home, just the week or so before.

Chapter 5

The Minister and the Selkie's Grave...

It was a cold, frosty afternoon and Colin had just finished the committal of 'old Jock' aka John MacDonald of A' Chàrnaich Farm, and was walking back through the graveyard when he saw the small grave of a child which he hadn't noticed before.

The inscription was written in strange lettering that Colin didn't recognise.

As he stood wondering what it might mean, a tall man, Norrie McLean, stopped and spoke to Colin. "Aye Meenister, it's a sad tale to be sure," he said and removed his cap in respect.

"Yes indeed, Mr McLean, a child's grave is always a sad sight."
"Aye, just that." Norrie agreed.
"What does it say?" Colin was keen to find out more about this sad little plot.

Norrie spoke with great reverence as he translated the engraved words ~

"The child's name was Lilly.

'Lilly'
"I am a Selkie child
No longer here to be.
My mother took me home
To my family 'neath the sea"

Colin felt an unexpected surge of sadness come over him and was close to tears.
"Oh my goodness, such a heart-rending verse."
He took a moment to compose himself and asked, "I've heard about them, but what actually *is* a Selkie?"
Norrie explained the age old story of the Selkies. "There are different accounts, but here on Rhua we say that Selkies are 'fallen angels' who come back as seals and they can transform into human likeness. They can be male or female. The males are extremely rugged and handsome, and the females are extremely seductive and beautiful.

They would marry a local girl or boy, have a child and live as any normal human family.
But in time, they cannot resist the call of the sea and always long to return to their home underwater.

It has been known for them to take their partner or child with them and are never seen again.
In the case of this wee one, she was said to be a Selkie child who lived in the village until she was seven years old when she died of a fever.
Her human father's family buried her here – but it is said that her Selkie mother returned to the sea and took wee Lilly with her. But no-one can be sure of the truth of it.

But every year on the date of her passing, her Selkie mother comes out of the sea and leaves flowers on her daughter's grave before returning heartbroken, into the water. Sometimes silver tears have been seen on the pathway back down to the shore. I've seen them for myself.
No-one on the Island has ever seen her, but

there is always a small bouquet of underwater flowers, sea anemone's and suchlike, left by her grave on 1st November, the same date as All Saints day, the day after All Hallow's eve."

Colin was lost for words, but after a few moments he said, "What a sad, yet beautiful story Mr McLean."

"Yes, but it's not just *any* story Meenister – it's a <u>true</u> story!"
Mr McLean was adamant that it was no fairy tale but a revered and respected part of Island life on Rhua.
"There are many accounts of Selkies being seen on Rhua, some lived among us for many years before returning to the sea. Lilly's family was one such family.

When Colin got home, he told Lorna all his about conversation with Mr McLean.
"Oh yes, I'd forgotten about poor wee Lilly, they say she had webbed feet."
"Mr McLean said that no one has ever seen the

mother who comes out from the sea. Has nobody ever hidden and watched for her?" asked Colin.

"Oh mercy, no! No one would think of doing such a thing, that would be most disrespectful. Everyone keeps away from the cemetery on that day, out of respect for the wee one and her sad mother."

As the weeks passed, Colin couldn't get the Selkies grave and the story of little Lilly out of his mind.

As the winter got colder and the frost bit deeper, the good people of Rhua 'battened down the hatches' against the cold winds which were coming down from the North.

In the Manse, Lorna threw another peat on the fire.

She looked out of the window, it was a cold, bare night. "There'll not be many guisers out tonight," she said.

"Oh, that's right, it's Halloween, I'd forgotten all about that." Colin shook his head.

He wasn't a big fan of Halloween, he didn't hold with the way that the once sacred festival of remembering those who had passed on, was being turned into a night of capers and carry-on's.

"Och, it's just harmless fun," said Lorna, trying not to get Colin started. "The lads of the village career around getting up to mischief, but it's only high spirits," she explained.

"And the big bonfire outside the hotel, what's _that_ all about?"
"It's something our ancestors have always done," Lorna explained. "It's to keep away evil spirits from the Island. Years ago they built _two_ bonfires and the people, sometimes with their cattle, would walk between them as a kind of cleansing ritual to keep them safe from evil spirits.

"_Praying_ would be a better way of asking for God's protection from evil spirits!" Colin said with conviction.

"Aye, you're right dear." She knew what Colin's views were and thought it best not to wind him up.

"And, of course, tomorrow is All Saints Day," Lorna said, hoping to cheer Colin up.

"So it is. Is that not wee Lilly's birthday?" Colin seemed to remember.

"I think it is, now you mention it, poor wee mite." Lorna answered.

"I wonder if her mother will leave the usual flowers on her grave this year.

I have Mr McAskill's funeral the day after tomorrow, I'll take a wee look at her grave while I'm at the cemetery."

"Och Colin, I wish you wouldn't." Lorna wasn't happy about Colin going to the little grave.

"It isn't right, gawping at the wee soul's final resting place."

"I won't gawp, I promise. I'll just be taking a wee look in the by-going, just out of curiosity."

"Colin Campbell, it's worse you're getting! You're beginning to sound like one of the old Island bodachs *(old men)!*"

Just at that, a great cloud of dark peat smoke billowed down the chimney, out of the hearth and into the room.

"What the blazes...?" Colin and Lorna jumped up. Colin ran through to the kitchen for a basin full of water to douse the fire, which only caused more smoke to rise from the hearth.

Colin wasn't a superstitious man but he had to admit to wondering if it wasn't some sign, some connection to him saying that he was going to visit Lilly's grave.

As they were taking it all in, they heard boisterous laughing outside and the sound of people running.

"I know what's going on!" Lorna said. "Some of the lads have put something heavy over the top of the chimney, it was something the boys used to do when I was young."

"The little bugg...." Colin stopped himself.

"Now, remember that you're a Meenister!" Lorna couldn't help but laugh.

Colin went up on the roof the next morning and Lorna had been right, there was a large peat on top of the chimney pot!

He mumbled to himself as he took it off and threw it down to the ground.

Lorna had to go back inside as she couldn't stop herself from laughing.

Two days later, as Colin was leaving the Cemetery after Mr McAskill's interment, he was determined not to go over to wee Lilly's grave. *'It would be improper to 'gawp' at the wee grave, just as Lorna said.'*

But as he was going over it in his mind, he found himself walking by the child's grave.

"Oh well, now I'm here it won't do any harm to take a wee look I suppose," he convinced himself.

As he came closer to the tiny grave he looked down to see the most beautiful posy of flowers of coral pink, red, yellow and green sea flowers, all tied up with strands of sea grass.

His heart missed a beat as he saw flakes of 'silver tears' around the grave and scattered along the path and through a tiny gate which led to the sea shore. Colin followed them down to the water's edge.

Were they 'silver tears' or fish scales? He couldn't say but as he picked one up it dissolved (*or did it 'disappear?'*) in his hand.

He felt a sense of guilt that he had somehow violated little Lilly's resting place - and he closed his eyes and prayed for forgiveness.

As he walked away from Lilly's grave he said quietly, "Sleep in peace, little one," and left the cemetery with a heavy heart.

He never told Lorna what he had done, and Lorna never asked, but he knew that he had come across something very special, something beautiful, something 'other worldly' – and he concluded that there are some things which are better left – unexplained…

Chapter 6

The Meenister goes Fishing…

It was a dreich day as mist and heavy rain swept across the remote little island of Rhua. Colin was in Mr Ali's convenience shop looking along the shelves for Custard Creams, when a voice behind him said, "That's the weather back to normal then, Meenister." It was John Angus *(his 'Sunday' name)* aka 'Bumper,' who worked for the council's roads department.

"Aye John Angus, it's not a day to be out," Colin said as he located the Custard Creams.
"You're right Meenister, even the midgies keep their heads down on a day like this!"
"Well, that's a blessing at least!" Colin laughed.
"Aye, just that," Bumper replied, not too sure if it was okay to laugh about blessings and the like.

Unknown to Colin, Bumper was a prolific poacher and had taken a bet from a group of his pals, for £5, that he couldn't talk the new Meenister into going poaching with them.

"No bother at all!" he had said to his pals, "I'll have him pulling in the net before you know it." This brought great hilarity from his friends which only served to strengthen his determination to win the bet.

For Bumper, it wasn't about the fish or the money, but a matter of personal pride.

A few minutes later, as Colin continued to scan the shelves for the other items that Lorna had asked him to pick up, Bumper stepped out in front of him again.

"Ah, we meet again, Meenister," Bumper said, "How are you keeping?"

"Just as fine as I was a few minutes ago when I last spoke to you." Colin was puzzled as their previous encounter regarding the rain and the midgies was just a matter of a few minutes ago in the previous aisle.

"Oh, yes, so we did," Bumper mumbled.

"Are you alright?" Colin enquired. Bumper's

behaviour was very strange, or so it seemed to Colin, but of course, he was trying to engage the Minister in a conversation and lure him into going 'fishing' with him, and so, winning the bet.

"No, no, I'm fine Meenister, I just wondered…er..if you… er…would like to go fishing one day, well, night actually, the fish bite better at night, you see."
"Fishing?" Colin asked.
"Yes fishing, you know, with a rod and reel, well, sometimes with a net, to save the fish from getting too stressed, as a kindness to them." Bumper was rambling by this stage.

Taken aback, Colin said, "Well, I don't know, I'd never really thought about it but…"
"Oh, you'll love it. You'll never know if you don't try it." Bumper was persistent.
"That's true I suppose – when were you thinking of going? Not today in this rain, I hope." Colin didn't much like the idea of being out in the heavy Rhua rain with no shelter.

"Maybe we could wait for a good day?" Colin suggested.

"Aye, that would be good, any day that suits yourself." Bumper felt he was successfully reeling the Minister in.

"Okay, but of course, not on a Sunday." Colin added.

"Oh, mercy no, Meenister! The Lord wouldn't be happy with us fishing on the Sabbath Day!" Bumper realised that he was overplaying the 'good Christian' thing, *especially as he hadn't been in church since he was in Sunday school*, so he stopped talking.

Colin looked at Bumper and asked, "Are you *sure* you're alright?"

Bumper feigned a sore head and left the shop saying he would get in touch soon.

Colin shook his head, wondering if Bumper really *was* okay, he seemed a little tense.

He thought no more about it, until a week or so later when he accidentally ran into Bumper in the village.

Well, I say, 'accidentally,' but it was more of a choreographed collision by Bumper who had followed Colin and then walked straight into him outside the Post Office.

"Oh dear! I'm sorry Meenister, I must have been daydreaming and didn't see you there." He had his hands in his pockets with fingers crossed.

"Don't worry John Angus, I was away in a dwam *(Dream)* myself. How are you, have you been fishing lately?"

"Funny you should say that Meenister, I was planning a cast or two before long, are you still up for the craic?"

"Oh, well, I'm sort of quite busy just now." Colin said with his fingers crossed behind his back.

"Oh, but this is the perfect time for it! The fish are fair jumping, just begging to be caught. How about tomorrow night, what do you say?"

"Well, um, okay then, where will I meet you?" Colin asked.

"How about we meet at Bridge End, by the wee metal bridge just at the back of the Hotel, at say,

11 o'clock?"

"In the morning?" Colin asked.

"No, in the evening. Meenister, it should be dark enough by then."

"But why does it have to be dark?"

"Oh, well….er… it's so the fish don't see us coming." Bumper automatically crossed his fingers again as he spoke.

"And it saves them from getting stressed."

"Oh right," Colin wasn't fully convinced but agreed to meeting up as planned.

"Oh, and there'll be a few of the lads there too, just in case we have a good haul and they will help us carry the fish up the road."

Bumper felt bad lying to a Meenister, *'I'm surely going to hell in a hand cart,'* he said to himself, but his feelings of guilt didn't last for long. At least he would win his bet with his pals and consoled himself knowing that the £5 was better in *his* pocket than in theirs.

"What about a rod, will I need to take one with me?" Colin asked.

"Don't worry, Meenister, I'll take everything we need, see you there," and Bumper hot footed it up the road before Colin could change his mind.

And so, it was all arranged. What could possibly go wrong?

All the next day Colin had a feeling of apprehension but wasn't quite sure why.
As Colin and Lorna were chatting over their evening meal she asked, "Is it tonight that you are going fishing?"
"Yes, I could do without it but Bumper is quite keen on it."
"But why do you have to go fishing at night?" Lorna asked.
"I asked Bumper that and he said it was so the fish wouldn't see us coming. Seems unlikely to me."

"Mmm, I think you'll need to keep your eye on Bumper!" Lorna had heard rumours about him. "He's a bit of a rogue by all accounts."
"Och Lorna, don't be listening to the gossips,

he seems a nice lad, I'm sure he is just being friendly and offering to take me fishing out of the goodness of his heart."

"Aye, maybe." Lorna wasn't so sure.

Later that evening, Colin got himself ready for his 'night outing with the boys.'
He came through from the scullery dressed in wellington boots, oilskin jacket and leggings, scarf and a Glasgow Rangers, red, white and blue, 'bobble hat.'

Lorna struggled not to laugh. "Oh, here comes Nanook of the North! Is it the North Pole that you are going?"

Colin had never been fishing before, except when he was about 5 years old with his Uncle Frank, his father's brother, and that was with a little net on a bamboo cane.
"I've got my pyjama's on under my waterproof leggings for extra warmth!"
Lorna couldn't control herself and started to giggle.

"What's so funny?" Colin asked.

"Nothing sweetheart, I'm sure the boys will have their jammies on under their trousers too."

"I don't see what's so funny, it's only being sensible. What if I caught a bad cold, it wouldn't be so funny then, would it?"

He looked like a lost little boy, and Lorna saw just how out of place he was in the Island setting. He was a city lad and not at all used to country ways – but she loved him all the more for it.

"I'm sorry, you look fine, prepared for any eventuality, very sensible," And she went over and hugged him. "I love you Colin Campbell. Now, you'd better be going or the lads might be getting a wee chill waiting for you."

They both laughed, even although Colin wasn't sure what was so funny, after all, the boys might just get cold if he kept them waiting too long.

It was a bright moonlit night as he arrived at Bridge End where Bumper and three other lads were waiting. Bumper saw him coming and thought, *"Yes! That's me £5 better off!"* His pals would have to pay up now.

He stepped forward and said, "You made it Meenister, that's great. This is Torquil, Kenny and Fin, short for Finlay, to give him his Sunday name.

We'll head up river, there's a pool in a mile or so, we'll catch a few there for sure. Here, hold this." He gave Colin a canvass bag and led the way along the riverside path.

"What's in the bag? Colin asked as they walked.

" That's the net."

"Net? Where are the fishing rods?" Colin was confused.

"I'll explain how it works once we get to the pool."

They walked on for a good bit before Bumper stopped. "Okay, Torquil and Fin, you stay here, you know what to do. Meenister, Kenny, follow me," and he climbed down an embankment and walked along the riverside for a hundred yards or so until they came to a pool.

"Okay, Meenister, you take one end of the net and walk round to the other side of the pool and be careful now. Kenny will hold on to this end and stretch the net across the pool. Then I'll go up to Torquil and Fin and they'll do their bit."
Colin was completely mystified as to what was going on.
"Okay, let's go before Bookem gets wind of it."
Colin could hear the distant sound of alarm bells ringing.

"Go Meenister! We don't have all night!"
Colin gingerly made his way round to the other side of the pool and stood on a flat rock as Kenny and Bumper pulled it tightly across the width of the small pool. Bumper scrambled his way back towards the other lads and said, "Ok boys!" in a loud whisper.
Kenny looked over at Colin, nodded and said, "Hold tight Meenister!"
Suddenly there was a mighty sound as Torquil and Fin started to thrown rocks into the river.
Colin wondered what on earth was going on.

The plan was that the fish would be panicked into fleeing down stream and straight into Colin and Kenny's waiting net!

After a few minutes, Torquil, Fin and Bumper appeared and helped them haul in the net – it was a good haul.

As they dragged the net on to the bank and began gathering the fish into bags, quite unexpectantly a large, bright torchlight shone from behind them and a booming voice shouted out, "Okay boys, I've got you red-handed this time – the game's up - drop the fish!"

It was PC Bookem!

In the words of the old saying – *'All hell was let loose!'*

Bookem bellowed, "Don't move, you're all for the high jump this time!"

"Run lads, it's Bookem!" Bumper shouted.

Colin was horrified! He imagined what the ladies of the village would say, *"The Meenister, arrested for Poaching, and him a man of the cloth, whatever next!?"*

The boys ran in all directions to confuse Bookem.

The moon, as if by divine intervention, was momentarily covered by a passing black cloud, and in the darkness, Colin decided to remove himself before it was too late, and he ran downstream for all he was worth, back to the Manse.

Bookem sneaked up behind Bumper, who held a large Salmon in his hand, and before Bookem could grab him, Bumper swung round and hit Bookem a mighty blow in the chest and knocked him flat!
Seeing that Bookem was winded, Bumper slipped a few more fish into his bag, picked up his net and ran off into the darkness.

Back at the Manse, Colin ran in the back door, across the kitchen and into the bedroom, slamming the door behind him.
Lorna woke up with a start, "Whatever's going on!?"

"It's Bookem. He's after me!" said Colin, shivering behind the bedroom door.

He explained all that had happened. "Imagine if word gets out that I was caught poaching! It doesn't bear thinking about!"

"Calm down sweetheart. Did PC Bookem see you?"

"I don't think so, he may have got a hold of Bumper but I was on my way by then. Oh dear, what am I to do?"

Colin was beside himself with worry.

"What if Bookem finds out!?"

"Don't you be worrying yourself sweetheart, if Bookem didn't see you and the boys are certainly not going to say anything or it will incriminate themselves, so you are safe enough."

"Okay sweetheart, and you were right about Bumper, sorry. He's a rogue for sure."

Lorna began to see the funny side of it and began to laugh. "What's so funny?" Colin said.

"Imagine, here's me thinking that I was married to a law abiding Meenister but now it seems I am married to a man who is on the run from the law!" Lorna giggled.

It took a moment, but soon Colin could see the funny side of it too.

He slept well that night, after all, it *was* quite exciting!

They rose late the next morning and were having a quiet morning when, just before lunchtime, there was a knock on the Manse door, it was PC Bookem!

Colin began to panic, perhaps Bookem had come to arrest him!

"Stay calm sweetheart, I'll get the door and you put the kettle on." Lorna said in her most reassuring voice.

She tried to look surprised, "Oh, it's yourself, come away in, Colin is just putting on the kettle, you'll take a wee cuppa now you're here?"

"Oh yes, thank you. I am needing it after the night I have had."

"Oh dear, has something happened? Perhaps a dram might help?" said Lorna. "Sweetheart, will you pour PC Malcolm a dram, he's saying he's had a fair night of it!"

"Nothing serious, I hope," Colin asked.

"Serious enough Meenister, serious enough," said Bookem.

"It's a terrible thing when a man of the Law is physically attacked in person while he is in the line of his duty!"

"Goodness me, what happened? Take a seat and tell us all about it." Colin was beginning to relax as he poured a dram for Bookem and took a quick one for himself too.

"Well, I can't break any discrechancies, for legal reasons, you understand."

"Of course, we quite understand, do go on." Lorna was eager to hear his version of events.

"It was a rough gang that set about me last night! Up from Glasgow no doubt, they were an ugly looking bunch, to be sure."

"From Glasgow you say?" Lorna had the devil in her and winked at Colin. Of course, *he* was from Glasgow.

"Aye, and there was 10 or 12 of them at least. I wouldn't be surprised if they were well known to the Inter-Polis."

"Goodness me! What happened, are you okay?"

"I've been watching the river for some time now. Poachers are taking the fish by the barrow load, it's big business down south.

Well, I was out on the prowl last night when I heard the blighters throwing rocks into the river, and there were others holding the net, nasty pieces of work they were!

As I crept up on them, the balloon went up and they ran in all directions.

I grabbed one but he attacked me and knocked me over and left me for dead!"

"That's terrible, did he punch you? How awful for you."

"Well, no he didn't actually *punch* me he, er, he..."

"He what? What did he do to you, John?"

"He hit me with a fish!"
Lorna and Colin looked at each other and had to turn away for fear of laughing out loud.

"He hit you with a fish?" Colin recapped.
"He did that, it was big fish too, a four or a five pounder I'd say. It fair took the wind out of me."
"Poor thing!" Lorna was genuinely sorry for him, he was certainly distressed by the whole episode.
"Aye Lorna, you wouldn't get that in Ballachulish!" PC Bookem said as he knocked back his dram in one smooth action and continued. "But I'll get the ringleader – I saw him running off and I'd recognise him again."
Colin froze. "How…how…would you recognise him?"
"He had on a red, white and blue striped hat with a wee bobble on the top!
I didn't see his face, but I'd could identify that hat in a line up a mile away!"

Lorna looked over Bookem's shoulder and there, lying on the draining board, was Colin's woolly red, white and blue hat, complete with bobble on the top!

She tried nodding over towards the sink, but Colin didn't catch on.

"Oh, Colin, why not get PC Malcolm another dram and don't forget the _water_." She said, nodding and winking over towards the sink.

Colin suddenly saw it. "Oh, gosh, yes, okay sweetheart."

He poured another dram and went over to the sink to put a splash of water in it, stuffing the hat under the sink at the same time, and then handed Bookem his second dram.

"I shouldn't really, I'm on duty, but it's calming my nerves, so it's kind of medicational I suppose."

"Aye, it will do you good, and besides, there's no ferry today so you know that Sergeant Galbraith won't be doing one of his 'surprise' visits from Oban, today."

"Aye, okay then, Meenister, you have talked me into it, I'll take another, thank you.
The Sergeant's surprise visit is not until next Tuesday anyway." And he knocked back his dram in one swift gulp.

PC Bookem was getting quite relaxed by this time, and out of the blue he asked Colin, "Have you ever seen a 'splash net,' Meenister?"
Lorna was at the sink and froze. She dropped a plate into the sink – and Colin dropped his custard cream which landed in his cup of tea that was sitting on the kitchen table.
Was it a trick? Was Bookem trying to catch Colin off guard?
"No, I er, don't think so, what is…. a splosh net?"
"A splash net, Meenister, *splash*, net."
Bookem went on to explain how two men hold a net across the river while others throw rocks in further up stream, and the commotion sends the fish down and right into the net.

Colin looked surprised. "Oh right. So *that's* how it works? Mercy me, how fascinating, who would believe it, goodness gracious, well I never."

Lorna intervened before Colin gave himself away.

"Would you stay for lunch, John? There's enough for us all, and some left over for you to take home for your tea." Lorna asked.

"Well, that's very kind of you, what are you having?"

Lorna and Colin looked at each other, smiled and said in unison ~

"Poached Salmon......!"

Chapter 7

The Minister and the Banshee…

Foreword : *The Banshee is a supernatural being from Celtic folklore which takes the form of an old, wailing woman or hag (Cailleach) who forewarns of an impending death.*

*

It was a cold, dark night in Kinlochmhor and the snow was blowing from the North, straight off the Arctic snow fields, across the North Sea, covering the little Hebridean Island with a deep, white carpet. The howling winds were blowing up a storm.

"The temperature is fair dropping," Colin said as he threw another peat on the fire.

"Aye, I pity anyone who is out on a night like this." Lorna replied.

Just at that, there was a faint knocking on the front door.

"Who on earth…?" Colin started to say when the knocking came again but it was louder and seemed more urgent this time.

He opened the front door and was taken aback to find that there was no-one there.

As he leaned out to look around, not only was there no-one to be seen, but even stranger - there were no footprints in the deep snow around the croft either.

"Who is it?" called Lorna.

"Well, um, no-one," replied Colin.

Lorna came to see for herself.

"See, no-one," Colin repeated.

"And no footprints…" Lorna noticed.

A chill ran down her spine, "Shut the door! Quickly!" she said with a sense of urgency and went and sat by the fire – Colin could see that she was shaking and unsettled.

"Are you okay, sweetheart?" he asked.

"Aye, I'm fine," Lorna answered but he knew she was anxious about something.

"What is it?" Colin insisted.

"Do you know what the date is?" Lorna asked.

"No, what has the date got to do with anything?"

"It's the 25ᵗʰ of March, a bad day…"
"Ah yes, the 'Cailleach's day'," Colin said with a smile.
"Latha na Cailleach *(the day of the Cailleach)* is nothing to joke about!" Lorna said sharply.
"Oh dear, what's upsetting you sweetheart?"
"Well, you'll think it's silly, but… but… did you hear the voice outside?"
"You mean, the wind? It was just the wind howling, it's pretty wild out there!"

"Yes, I heard the wind – but there was another sound, a voice, a wailing, weeping voice, blowing through the wind, did you not hear it?"
Colin was unsure what to say. He was aware that Lorna had the 'gift' and could see, feel and hear things that most people couldn't, and he could see that she was troubled by whatever she had heard.
So, rather than cause any further upset he said, "It's getting late sweetheart, how about we have a wee dram to keep out the cold, and turn in?"
And that's just what they did.
Lorna had a restless night, between the visions, the voices and the tossing and turning, she

finally had to give in and get up.

She looked at the bedside clock, it was 3am as she tiptoed out of the bedroom and went through to the kitchen.

A while later, Colin sensed that Lorna wasn't beside him and he rose and went through to the kitchen where he saw Lorna sitting at the table with a cup of cold tea in front of her.

"Are you alright sweetheart?" he asked her. "You'll catch your death of cold sitting here, come back to bed and get warmed up."

"But Colin, you don't understand, the wind, the voice – it was faint but I know it was the Ban Shee! I have heard her wailing before, many years ago, she is warning of a death!"

He knew enough to know that Lorna was not hallucinating or imagining things, he only had to look at her face to see that she was deadly serious.

"I don't know what to say sweetpea, but we can only wait and see. If there *is* to be a sad passing, then there's nothing we can do, except pray for the unfortunate family. Let's get back to bed sweetheart and try to get some sleep – and we'll see what tomorrow brings."

The wind continued to howl throughout the night, bringing a troubled sleep to them both.

The next morning was a glorious morning, with deep snow and bright sunshine.

"How are you feeling this morning?" Colin asked Lorna.

"A bit better, thank you. That wind really unsettles me, it always has, but I am quite sure I heard a voice calling through the storm."

"Well, there's been no calls about a death on the Island, PC Bookem usually calls me if there is. So hopefully it's a false alarm."

The day had been quiet as the unusually heavy snowfall had kept most of the Islanders indoors. Indeed, it was a further three days before things started to move around the island.

Many of the older folk said that they hadn't seen snow quite like it for many years.

"Aye, the last time we had snow like this, a dark shadow covered the island for weeks," said

Lorna, ominously.

She was referring to the time in March 1907 when there had been a great sickness in many Scottish cities. A passing boat from Glasgow is said to have inadvertently brought a dreadful infection to the island as they sheltered from a Storm, and death had visited a number of the islanders.

"Oh dear, how awful," Colin said solemnly, let's pray that doesn't happen again. At least there haven't been any phone calls from PC Bookem, so that's a good thing. Would you like a cup of tea?"

Lorna was just about to say, "That would be good…" when the phone rang.
They looked at each other and thought the same thing – *'it can't be, can it?'*
Colin picked up the receiver.

He put his hand over the mouthpiece and whispered to Lorna, "It's Bookem!"
'Now that is spooky!', they both thought.

"Is that yourself that's speaking, Meenister?" Bookem asked.

"Yes, it's myself that's speaking," replied Colin with a smile.

He loved Bookem's quaint way of speaking 'the English' (a' bruidhinn Beurla), but of course English was his second language, as it was for the majority of the Islanders.

"What can I do for you John? I hope no-one has passed on."

"No, Meenister." Lorna heard Bookem's words and breathed a sigh of relief.

"But there is no reply from old Mrs McKenzie over at Sgitheach Croft (Hawthorn Cottage).

The wee road over to her croft is blocked with snow, so we're putting together a search party to go over and see if she is alright, and I was wondering, with you being the Meenister and all, if you would like to come with us? Dr Livingston will be with us to, just incase, well, you know, in case she has passed on to greater glory, if you know what I mean."

"Yes, I know what you mean John, but surely it's more likely that the phone line is down, with the snow."

"Well, Meenister, that's as could be, but she doesn't have the phone in, and besides that, I would be diuretic in my duty if I don't go and find out."

"Yes, you're quite right John, when are you leaving?"

"In about ten minutes, are you up for it? We'll come round by for you shortly," Bookem said and abruptly hung up.

"Oh my goodness, did you hear that?" Colin asked Lorna.

"Yes, so you'd better hurry up and get changed into your warm clothes, and don't forget to put your pyjama trousers on under your oilskin leggings."

There was a frenzy as Colin ran around trying to find his warmest clothes and get dressed. Within just a few minutes they heard a Tractor pulling up outside the Manse.

There was a trailer in tow with Dr Livingstone and four of the local 'lads' in the back, all (apparently) fortified by strong drink. Probably just to keep out the cold.

"Come on Meenister, don't dilly dally on the way, now," shouted one of the lads, which was followed by loud laughter.

"They certainly seem in good spirits," Colin said to Lorna as he kissed her on the cheek and set off down the path.

"Aye, '*Spirits*' *is* the word for it, right enough," she thought to herself as she closed the front door, shaking her head.

It took Bookem and his 'merry band' about an hour to reach Sgitheach Croft, a journey that would normally have taken less than half of that time when the roads were clear of snow.

When they arrived, the first thing that struck them was that there were no footprints in the snow around the Croft.

On entering the little home, they called out but there were no signs of Mrs McKenzie, only an eerie silence.

As they looked into each room, it was as if she had just walked out and left things as they were. The kettle was still on the range, a cup and saucer were in the sink, unwashed. In the small front room, a half eaten scone and a cold cup of tea were on a small table beside Mrs McKenzie's chair.

Things were beginning to feel uncomfortable for the lads, something didn't seem quite right.

"We'd better take a look outside," Bookem said. "If the Minister, Alec Angus and Murdo John look in the buildings out the front – Donnie, young Fin and myself will take a look around the back of the croft and byre. Doctor, maybe you would stay here and check the house."

Everyone was impressed with Bookem's organising skills, until he said, "Okay, let's synchromesh watches. I make it half past ten."

"Well, I make it twenty past ten," said Donnie.

"And I don't have a watch at all!" Alec Angus replied.

"Och, never mind the synchromeshing, just get going. Back here in 15 minutes!"

Bookem remembered organising a similar search party going out on the hills when he was a village Bobby in Argyll a number of years ago, and he shook his head and thought, *"You'd never get this sort of thing in Ballachulish!"*

Just as they were about to split up and head out, a loud bark came from one of the bedrooms.
"Mercy me, it's Corran! I'd know that bark anywhere," said Dr Livingstone.
Sure enough, when they looked under the bed, Corran was cooried under a blanket in the corner – and he didn't want to come out.

"Leave it to me boys, I have a way with dogs," said Fin.
"Aye, he's *gone to the dogs* more like!" Alec Angus quipped, much to the amusement of the others.

"Stand back! I'm going in!" Fin said dramatically as he crouched down and looked under the bed.

"What's the matter boy? Where's mummy then?"

The lads looked at each other…trying not to laugh.

Suddenly Corran sprang and bit Fin's finger!

"Ya wee bugg.." Fin shouted.

"Now, now, watch the language young Fin. It's the Meenister that is standing behind you!" Bookem remarked.

"Ha ha, aye, it's a great way you have with the dogs right enough, Fin!" Donnie joked.

"Well, I wasn't expecting the 'Hound from Hell' to attack me!"

Colin went into the kitchen and searched the cupboards for biscuits. He came upon a tin with a couple of Custard Creams in. *'Good choice, Mrs McKenzie!'* he said to himself.

He crushed up a biscuit and made a wee trail out from under the bed, and coaxed Corran to come out.

He was a small, frightened Terrier, not much more than a puppy. Colin picked him up and

Corran licked his face.

"Ha, ha, some Hound from Hell!" Alec Angus said, and everyone laughed, everyone except Fin, that was!

Dr Livingston said, "Yes, and from what I know about Corran from my occasional home visits to Mrs McKenzie, is that he would never leave her side."

"So, where is she, then?" Fin asked no-one in particular.

"Not far away, I'll wager, Dr Livingston replied.

"Well, if that's the case, we had better get looking! Let's go - and leave no stone unturned! Back here in 15 minutes!" PC Bookem said with an air of urgency.

As if listening to the conversation, Corran made for the back door and stood there scratching the door and whining.

"Looks like the wee fellow is trying to tell us something, open the door Donnie," Bookem said.

As Donnie opened the back door, Corran got his wee nose in the gap of the open door and flew out across the yard, under the fence and made a bee-line for a small stone building a few hundred yards away. It had once been used for keeping lambs in at springtime, but Mrs McKenzie, like other families, now used it as a cold store.

"Over here boys, she's in here!" Alec Angus shouted and dashed in after Corran.

He found poor Mrs McKenzie lying on the ground, as white as the snow outside, with wee Corran lying close beside her.

"Look at the wee fellow, he's trying to keep her warm, but I fear it might be too late." Fin said gravely.

Dr Livingston came in and immediately knelt down and searched for any vital signs of life.

After a few minutes, he took off his stethoscope and shook his head saying, "She is extremely cold and I reckon she's been lying here for two, maybe three days, and there's no sign of a pulse, sorry boys."

The little group fell silent.

"I think it's time for a prayer," said Colin, and

they all nodded and bowed their heads.

Colin gave thanks for her life and was about to ask for God's mercy and Grace when Dr Livingston shouted, "She blinked! I can't detect a pulse, but I saw her blink!"

He pressed his stethoscope to her chest but still couldn't detect a heartbeat.

"She blinked again, I saw her!" Donnie shouted excitedly.

"Me too!" said Colin.

Just at that, Mrs McKenzie coughed and opened her eyes!

"She's alive, praise the Lord!" exclaimed Bookem, "She is back from the brink!"

There was a great feeling of relief and thanksgiving among the group.

"We'd better get her across to the house," Dr Livingstone said, and as Donnie and Fin lifted her up, Colin took off his gloves and put them on her ice cold hands.

PC Bookem led the way. "Careful now!" he said about every other step, as the boys struggled to carry her through the knee deep snow.

Wee Corran jumped and barked alongside and managed to wiggle his way through the snow back to the croft.

They laid Mrs McKenzie on her bed and threw blankets over.

"Meenister, would you get the kettle on and make a hot cup of tea for herself - and perhaps find something a bit more 'energetic' to warm us all up. Tea is fine, but occasions like this demand something more substantial."

Fin and Alec Angus went through with Colin to lend a hand.

"You'll find a bottle of the 'good stuff' in the cupboard above the sink," Dr Livingstone said helpfully. "She keeps it handy, for medicinal purposes." Everyone smiled. *Trust Dr Livingstone to know where the bottle was kept!'*

Corran scrambled up on to the bed and lay full length beside Mrs McKenzie.

They found a bottle of 12 year old Glenlivet *(the*

'good stuff' that Dr Livingstone had mentioned) and were tempted to take a wee snifter themselves, but they all new that wouldn't be right without Mrs McKenzie's say so, but perhaps…under the circumstances…?

About 5 minutes or so later, the warm tea had worked its magic (*or was it the '12 year old' added ingredient?*) - and Mrs McKenzie stirred and opened her eyes.

"Oh, mercy me!" she said and looked around.

"For a moment I thought I might be in Heaven, but I see PC Bookem and the Meenister there, so it can't be!" The boys laughed.

"Aye, she's going to be fine," said Dr Livingstone.

"Thanks be to God," Colin said, and everyone nodded in agreement.

"Well done boys, you've done a grand job." Bookem said.

Corran popped his head out of the covers and gave a single bark, as if to say, *'what about me"*

Aye Corran, you too! You saved a precious life today, well done!"

They all clapped as Corran snuggled back under the covers.

Mrs McKenzie had a tear in her eye as she said, "Thank you all *so* much."

"But what were you doing outside on such a wild night?" Bookem asked.

"I heard the Banshee wailing and was sure it was myself she was calling, so I went outside to chase her away but there was no-one there."

"Mercy! Were you not afraid, Mrs McKenzie?" asked Fin.

"Certainly not! I knew the good Lord would protect me. But I tripped and fell over and managed to crawl in here, out of the snow. It was then I was sure that I heard the Lord calling me. I wasn't frightened or worried as I knew I would be in Paradise and safe in His holy hands. But it wasn't to be."

"It wasn't your time, Mrs McKenzie," Colin said, "He will call you in His own good time, not before." And everyone said, 'Amen.'

Later that day, Colin was telling Lorna all that had happened.

"See, I told you I heard the Banshee a few nights ago!" said Lorna.

"But it couldn't have been sweetheart, Mrs McKenzie didn't die, she is very much alive, thank God," Colin replied with some satisfaction.

Lorna wasn't sure what to say – but just then the phone rang. Colin answered. It.

"Oh, hello John." *'It's Bookem'*, he whispered to Lorna.

"Oh dear, a death? Who was it?" Colin asked.

Lorna's ears pricked up.

"And when was this…?"

"About three days ago…?"

"The night of the really bad snow? I see." And

he looked over at Lorna who gave him a, *'I told you so'* kind of look.

"Okay, thank you for letting me know John, I'll

pop over and see the family in the morning," and he hung up.

"Has there been a passing, sweetheart?" Lorna asked.
"Yes, Mr Grant from Lochan Farm. His daughter found him lying out in the barn, stiff as a board he was."

"Would that be the same night as the heavy snowfall a few days ago?" Colin knew where this was leading.

"Oh, I think so, yes," Colin said, knowing he was being walked into a trap.
"Will that be the same night as I heard the Banshee, then?"
"Oh yes, I had forgotten about that!" Colin crossed his fingers behind his back. "It could be, I suppose."
"Colin Campbell, you know fine well I heard the Banshee on the same night as Mr Grant's passing! Admit it!"

Colin laughed, "Alright sweetpea, I admit it, it was the very same night."

"So, I wasn't imagining it then?"

Colin felt that Lorna was milking it now.

"No sweetheart, you didn't imagine it.'

"So I was right then?" Lorna continued.

"Yes, you were right, as usual," Colin replied with a cheeky smile.

"Am I not *always* right?" Lorna said with a laugh.

"Don't push your luck!" Colin replied with a grin.

"Och, am I not just pulling your leg sweetheart?" Lorna said, smiling. "Would you like another cup of tea and the last custard cream?"

"Okay, seeing as it's yourself that is asking," Colin said.

"Oh Colin, you are sounding more like one of the local Bodachs every day!"

"Aye, just that," he said," Just that," and he closed his eyes and smiled a contented smile.

Chapter 8

The Minister and the Haunted Croft…

It was a long, cold winter on the Inner Hebridean Island of Rhua.

When it *did* snow, which wasn't often, it usually didn't lie for long because of the salt air, but this winter the snow seemed to have been lying around for weeks.

The cattle had been taken in and the sheep were kept close by the croft.

The phone lines, such as they were, were down but it took a few days before anyone realised – they were often out of action due to the sheep chewing the connections.

Colin was carefully making his way home from a visit to the far side of the island to see Mrs McPhee who had recently lost her husband Danny.

The snow hadn't been too bad when he left Mrs McPhee's but now it was getting heavier, and

Colin found himself slipping left and right as he crawled along the little country road. It was getting dark and he was wondering if he would make it home that night.

As he came round the corner by old Jock McIvor's barn, the car ran right into a snow drift and ground to a halt.

Colin's heart was racing – what was he to do? He had never experienced snow like this in Glasgow.
Would he get out and walk? What if he were to get lost? Should he sit it out in the car? Perhaps he would freeze and not be found for days.

He looked around, it was dark and the snow flakes seemed to be getting bigger as they fell and covered the car like a soft, white blanket.
He was becoming anxious and began to fear the worst.

But then Colin thought he saw a light flickering up on the hillside – or was it his imagination?

He rubbed his eyes and looked again – yes, there it was, a light!

He got out of the car, pulled his collar up, climbed over the fence and made his way through the deep snow, towards the light.

As he was getting closer, he began to see the outline of a small croft and he was sure he had seen a woman standing by the door, wrapped in a shawl, beckoning him to come up to the croft. At least, he *thought* he was sure.

By the time Colin reached the croft there was no light and no-one there, it was just a dark, empty shell.

As he went inside, an uneasy feeling crept over him, but at least he was out of the cold and the snow for the night.

The night was as black as a bible with only the moon for light, but he managed to gather some loose straw and a couple of sacks which were lying around and cooried into a corner to keep warm.

Colin lay wondering who was the woman he saw waving at him earlier. *'Whoever she was,'* he thought, *'she led me to a safe place.'*

He tried to rationalise things by saying to himself, *'It must be the cold getting into me and giving me hallucinations,'* but he couldn't shake off a feeling of unease and anxiety.

As much as he tried to keep his eyes open and his wits about him, tiredness overcame him and before long he fell asleep.

*

Back at home, Lorna was worried that Colin hadn't returned home. The phone lines were down so she put on her coat and made her way down to the Police Station.

PC Bookem opened the door in his Police issue raincoat, Lorna could see his red striped pyjama's sticking out from his cuffs and trouser legs.

She told him her concerns, but Bookem was sure he would be somewhere safe.

"Now don't be worrying yourself young Lorna, the good Lord will be watching over him and he will have found a dry place to see out the night. "I'll get a few of the locals together and we'll go out at first light and search for him."

Lorna was comforted a little, but the morning was a few hours away yet. There was nothing else to do except go home and wait - and pray.

*

Colin slept fitfully for an hour or so when he was wakened by the sound of a woman crying. As he opened his eyes he could see an old woman in a rocking chair in the corner of the room, cradling a baby and sobbing uncontrollably. There was no sound from the little one.

It was his worst nightmare – meeting an apparition on a dark, winter's night. He didn't believe in ghosts but whoever she was, he could see her quite clearly.

After the initial shock, he composed himself and said, "Hello, is...is there something I can do to help?" The old lady didn't reply but continued to cry pitifully.

He was sure it was a dream but he knew he was awake. He closed his eyes, put his fingers in his ears and tried to will himself to sleep. Whenever he took a finger out of his ear, the crying continued.

He clenched his eyes tight, said a prayer and slept an uneasy sleep until first light.

In the morning, he tentatively opened his eyes and looked over to the corner of the room and was relieved to see that the old lady and the child were no longer there.

Colin heard shouting outside and the sound of a tractor engine running, he looked out of the window and saw PC Bookem standing on the running board of a tractor shouting, "Are you there Meenister? We are seeing your car but we're not seeing yourself! It's me, the Polis, with a rescue team."

Colin was mightily relieved, and he smiled when he saw who the 'rescue team' were – six of the local worthies, sitting in the trailer, some of whom he had previously crossed swords with about drinking in public on the Sabbath.

He could see that the sun was coming up and said to himself, *'Thank you Lord – I'm going to get home safely after all.'*

He looked around the room and thought, *'I must have been delirious, either that or I am losing the plot!'*

As he made for the door, he noticed a small piece of wood or bone, lying in the corner. It was about 4 inches long and carved into the shape of what looked like a fish or a seal, but it was very worn.

What could it be? He picked it up, put it in his pocket and set off down to the road.

On his way down the hill, he noticed two sets of footprints in the snow. One was obviously his own from last night as he came from the road – but who's were the other footprints? As he looked closer he could see that they came out of the croft doorway, turned past a big oak tree and went up the hill behind the croft, wound their way up through the snow and into a small clump of trees where the footprints stopped.

'Were they the old lady's?' Colin wondered. *'Should I go and follow the tracks or head home?'*

He was sure that Lorna would be worried about him, so he set off down the hill and resolved to return later to investigate.

He was greeted by 'the boys' who hoisted him up onto the trailer and handed him a bottle of 'the crater.'

"You'll be taking a wee dram Meenister, just for the medicational purposes of course - and besides, it's not the Sabbath today!"

Colin obliged, out of courtesy, and said, "Aye, you're awful lads, so you are - I'll say a wee prayer for you in church on Sunday!" They laughed, "Aye, Meenister," one said, "You'll do, you'll do!" and passed the bottle round, until it was empty.

*

When he got back home, Lorna was relieved to see him safe and in one piece. "Are you alright? I was so worried, where did you stay?" she asked, giving him a big hug.

He told her all that had happened, including the bit about the old lady and her footprints. He felt a bit foolish as he was sure it was all his imagination.

"What was the name of the croft?" Lorna asked.

"I'm not sure, but it was derelict and there was a big old oak tree beside the croft, I remember seeing that as I left this morning."

Lorna went as pale as a ghost. "A big oak tree, you say?"

'Yes, I thought it was a bit odd as there are no other oak trees around the island, at least not as far as I've seen."

"Are you sure it was an *oak* tree?"

"Yes, quite sure, it must be a very old one."

Lorna spoke slowly, "I know the croft you mean, it's called 'Croit na Darach' which loosely means 'the Croft of the Oak'. It was the scene of a sad incident many years ago, around 1747, or thereabouts.

A young girl came across to the island from the mainland, her name was Katy Campbell. She was expecting a child and her father had put her out of the house. Somehow, she made her way here, probably on a fishing boat out of Oban or perhaps Castlebay, no-one knows for sure.

She took up with a young man from Croit na Darach and the baby was born there. It was a sickly baby from birth. It was said that you could hear the mother's cries right across the island for days. Some said it was the ban-shee, warning of an imminent death.

Then suddenly one night, the crying stopped and mother and baby were never seen or heard of again. No bodies were ever found, nothing, it was a mystery.

The young man was arrested for murder and hung from the oak tree, although there was no proof. But perhaps now..." Lorna stopped, deep in thought.

"Are you thinking what I'm thinking?" Colin said, "That we should go to those woods and perhaps we will find the remains of mother and child, who were frozen in the winter snow of 1747?"

Lorna thought for a moment and said, "Would there be anything left to find now? And what would be gained if we *did* find something? Perhaps we should keep this to ourselves and let them rest in peace."

"Aye, maybe you're right," Colin agreed.

Then he remembered the small piece of bone that he had picked up and showed it to Lorna. "See what I found in the croft, any idea what it might be?"

Lorna looked and said quietly, "I know exactly what it is, it's a piece of deer horn and it's a very old babies dummy, a soother. In olden days they were often carved into the shape of an animal like a fish or a seal, like this one, for good luck, and to ward off evil spirits.

Sometimes it would be dipped into whisky, like an anaesthetic, and massaged into the child's gums when they were teething. No wonder so many on the island are fond of the whisky! It's a good job that my mother dipped mine into milk!

Colin smiled and said, "Aye, it would never do if the Minister's wife was pie-eyed most of the time! What would the good ladies of the village have to say about that!?"

They fell silent for a while, pondering the sad story of that poor mother and her tiny baby. They agreed that they would go and bury the small carved seal in the small clump of trees above Croit na Darach, once the weather had improved.

"Perhaps that will give the wee one some comfort after all these years," Colin said. "We'll take a walk up there when the snow is away and say a wee prayer."

A tear ran down Lorna's cheek, "What a lovely thought, that's just what we'll do."

After a few moments Lorna composed herself and said, "D'you fancy another Custard Cream sweetheart?"
"Oh yes please."
Colin never said *no* to a Custard Cream.

Chapter 9

The Minister and the 'Whisky Olympics'...

It was the first day of the Annual Rhua and District Gaelic Mod. There would be competitions for songs, poems, recitations, Highland Dancing and much more. It was a hub for all things Gaelic, and people would travel from near and far to compete, support or simply experience the unique atmosphere.

Last year there was a Gaelic skiffle band from the small Island of Eigg who called themselves, 'Eigg and Chips.' They nearly caused a riot when the lead singers' trousers fell down while hitting a particularly high note during their own version of, "A dram's a dram for a' that!"

This year, there was a record number of contestants in attendance and Rhua was awash with campers and travellers. Tents covered the Machair and just about every home had taken in a lodger or two for the week of the Mod.

"My goodness, what a swarm of incomers," observed Mrs Gass.

"Aye, Sandra, sure they're like the midgies, there's clouds of them everywhere!" replied her friend, Zena Fraser. "Sure, I was in Mr Ali's shop this morning and by the time I got to the front of the que, there were no rolls left and not a tea bag in sight!"

"Och, but they're harmless tho', didn't my brother Norrie not say the same thing?"

"Harmless!? Have you tried to get a half bottle of uisge *(whisky)* while the Mod is on? My cousin Murdo stocks up a few weeks before they come, just to be safe."

"But it's only for a week, Sandra."

"Aye, but a week is a fair sentence when there's no' a dram in the house!"

"Aye Sandra, just that," Zena had to agree.

It was Day 2 – and the Mod was now in full swing and already there had been controversy in the under 9 year old's children's singing competition. in the school hall.

Eight year old twins Jimmy and Jeannie Fraser had to be stopped mid verse as they innocently sang alternate verses of the old ballad, 'The Ball of Kirriemuir,' in the Gaelic.

At first, they appeared as sweet little angels – until they got into their routine.
The judges sat with mouths open and were horror-struck as the two little cherubs sang the song and added a little dance for effect.

"Where did you learn that song?" one of the Judges asked them. "Oh, it's a song that daddy sings when he comes home from the pub," said wee Jeanie. "Would you like us to sing the other verses for you?"
"No, no!.... that will be all for now, thank you."
Little Jimmy and Jeannie came down from the stage in tears for not being allowed to sing the rest of their father's favourite song.

Their father, *who was in the audience and fortified by strong drink,* stood up and harassed the judges so much that had to be escorted from the premises.

Day 3 - brought its own problems – two of the Gaelic choirs had chosen to sing the same song, 'Cailin Mo Ruinsa' *(The Maid I adore / Dearest, my own one)* and both choirs had, inadvertently, been scheduled to sing on the same day and at the same time.

'Quite easy to resolve,' you might think, however, both choirs were determined to sing at the same appointed time, resulting in both choirs standing on the stage, each refusing to leave.

After much negotiation, it appeared to have been settled when one elderly lady (who shall remain nameless) swung at an even more elderly gentleman and knocked his false teeth out.

"Well, he said that 'I sing like a strangled cat', I'm not standing for that!" she explained, at which a voice was heard to say, "No, he was quite wrong, a strangled cat is more in tune!"

One thing led to another which started what, in Glasgow parlance might be called 'a right old

Rammy'!

All Hades was let loose, and as there were about 20 singers in each choir, a riotous brawl ensued on stage, watched by an incredulous audience, which led to Scotland's finest, PC Malcolm aka Bookem, being called in to calm things down.

One gentleman had his toupé pulled off and an elderly lady had her walking stick broken in half, while the two choir conductors squared up in what the Oban Times dubbed, 'Mayhem at the Mod' with the snappy subtitle, 'A Rowdy Riot on Rhua!'

The judges were in shock.

"Is that not just terrible?" said Mr McCaulay the school teacher.

"Aye Colin, you wouldn't get this kind of thing in Ballachulish…" replied Mrs McColl, shaking her head in despair.

The judges all agreed that standards were fairly falling these days, and that it would never have happened in their day.

Day 4 - was a day of heavy rain, and in between competitions the majority of people either took shelter in the main shed (*aka old Sandy's byre*), for a cup of tea and some home baking, or went for a wee refreshment in the beer tent.

By mid afternoon they were 4 deep at the makeshift bar and the noise was getting noticeably louder.

Blood pressures were beginning to rise too as a large American gentleman, wearing full Highland Dress including a bright red beret with an extraordinarily large feather, fastened with a safety pin, was loudly proclaiming that he was fifty percent American Indian, twenty five percent Irish and twenty five percent Scottish as his great, great, great, great grandmother had come from 'Lock' Lomond.

"I wonder which part of him is Scottish," Lachie Campbell said.

"Probably his wallet, as he hasn't bought a round all day," one of the boys replied, much to the amusement of those close by.

The sun came out for a wee while in the afternoon but by now those in the beer tent felt obliged to remain where they were. "At least the wife will know where to find me," said Bernie Smith, *a well known character from Tiree.* "It'll save her having to worry about me getting lost." "Och, it's considerate that you are Bernie!" one of the local lads commented, "You would be as well to take a wee dram while you're waiting." "Aye, it'll keep out the damp," Bernie said thoughtfully, so another round of drams were taken. "Aye, the damp is a terrible thing, right enough," it was agreed.

"Slainte!" the little group said in unison as they each downed their dram in a 'one-er.'

Day 5 - saw the Highland Dancing and the individual Piping competitions, followed in the afternoon by the Adults and Children's Puirt à beul (*Porsht a beal* – ie mouth music) competitions.

Puirt à Beul is a style of singing, without music, usually fast and light hearted in content.

(This my favourite day of the Mod).

Mhairi Carmichael from Eilan Beg, a small island just a mile south of Rhua, was expected to win the Gold Medal, as she had for the past 10 years.

Because of her prolonged success, other competitors were reluctant to come forward, which meant that for the last 5 years Mhairi has been the only contestant. She was expecting to win again this year, being the only participant, but there had been a last minute name come forward, a young lady who had travelled up from Beauly, near Inverness, called Erin Moran.

Mhairi had thought she would automatically win again this year and had gone out with her friends the night before and had partaken of a number of Babyshams and Brandy.

Unfortunately. she must have been served a bad drink which made her most unwell the next morning, rendering her unable to sing.

However, not to be outdone, and determined to retain her title, Mhairi got up to sing the lovely Puirt à Beul song, *Fodor Dha Na Gamhna Beaga,'* which means, *'Fodder for the heifers when they would come in winter,'* but sadly, when she opened her mouth, only a loud croak erupted from her throat!

Poor Mhairi burst into tears and ran out of the hall, leaving Erin the only remaining competitor and so, by default, the winner.

Erin asked if she could be allowed to sing her song, the cheerful, *'Is Toigh Leam Fhìn Buntàta 's Ìm'*, which means, *'I, myself, like potatoes and butter.'* The judges conferred and agreed that as there was time available, she should be allowed to sing her song.

Soon the audience, even the judges, were clapping enthusiastically and tapping their feet to the catchy tune. It was a happy atmosphere, perhaps enhanced by the fact that someone else had, at last, won the *Puirt à Beul* Gold medal.

Day 6 – The sun was shining brightly and Colin and Lorna took a walk around the various events that were taking place in and around the village.

He had never been to a Mod before and was finding it quite an experience.

As he and Lorna walked about, they saw children playing, teenagers larking about and older folks catching up with each other's latest news – all communicating in their native tongue. Of course, it was all quite natural for them, but to Colin, coming from Glasgow, it was fascinating to see and hear.

There were choirs singing, pipers piping, singers singing and dancers dancing. It was a real cultural feast to the eyes and ears.

Lorna had been teaching Colin the Gaidhlig (Gaelic) and he was keen to try out his new found skills on some unsuspecting visitor.

As they ambled around, nodding here and there, he would try the occasional phrase which was usually met with a quizzical look and a blank stare.

"I think speaking the Gaelic with a Kelvingrove accent is mystifying the locals, Colin," Lorna said with a sympathetic smile. "Never mind sweetheart, we'll keep working on it and we'll have you speaking like 'Heeland Jock' before you know it."

It was the day for the under 13's and the under 19 year olds, 'Psalm Presenting' competitions.
It consisted of an individual singing (unaccompanied) the first line (or two, depending on local custom) of a Psalm, in the traditional Free Church manner, and a few members of their own congregation (no less than 6) will sing the part of the congregation.
"Oh, you'll love it Colin, it's so beautiful, especially with the young ones, their voices are like listening to the angels singing," said Lorna.

She wasn't wrong – the competition was a joy. The voices of the youngsters would put many professionals to shame as the harmony of the voices rose and fell like the waves of the sea, rising and falling on a beautiful, moonlit night.

*

Day 7 - The final day of the Rhua and District Gaelic Mod (*aka The Whisky Olympics*), was the day of the presentations.

Overall, it had been a great week, and the weather had been kind, mostly. Old friendships were rekindled, new friendships had been made, Drams had been taken, Cups were presented and Medals were awarded to the worthy recipients.

It was a day when many met up with old friends and much discussion took place about the marking of the judges and how the competitors from their own particular area were judges far too low and the others were marked too high.

The afternoon saw an interdenominational Gaidhlig Church Service and it was the custom of the Rhua Mod to round off the week with a final night Ceilidh – which was, for many, the highlight of the week.

It was the culmination of a week of Gaelic song, dance and verse, a time to let down the hair and rejoice in a united 'Dùthchas' (*Doo-khas*) - a mutual feeling of 'belonging' to the land, the language, a shared history, a shared faith, folklore and all that is 'the Gaeldom.'

It cannot be seen or touched, but rather felt and experienced in your heart and soul.

It awakens a sense of respect and courtesy for each other, which is exemplified by never refusing a dram when offered as it would be most impolite and discourteous to do such a dreadful thing!

The Ceilidh itself was full of fun and joy, wild dancing and enthusiastic twirling, skipping and laughter all rolled into one experience which was affectionally known as, 'A Grand Island Hooley.'

Strong drink was taken, in moderation of course, and it was agreed by all, that this year was the best Mod ever.

Slainte! Here's to next year!

Chapter 10

The Minister and the Witch's Cat...

One chilly afternoon the Reverend Colin Campbell was visiting an elderly Parishioner in the North end of the lovely isle of Rhua. It had been a nice spell of weather, and it was a good opportunity for him to get out and about on his BSA Gold Star motorbike.

The younger element of the islanders thought he was very trendy, but the older folk were less enthusiastic to see their Minister roaring about on a noisy motorbike.

"It's enough to put the cows off their feed," one senior gentleman remarked, "It's enough to waken the dearly departed," said another.

"It's against God's will to disrupt the peace and quiet of the good folk of Rhua," were all comments often heard around the Island, as Colin rode by.

This particular day he was visiting Mrs MacKinnon in her small croft called 'Torrach' *(which means 'fertile', as it was situated in a green*

and lush part of the Island which looked over the
Atlantic Ocean).

As he pulled up outside the croft, he saw Mrs MacKinnon draw back the curtain to see what all the noise was. By the time he had dismounted and taken off his helmet, she was standing at the door with her hands covering her ears.

As she spoke, she covered her mouth and said, "Oh mercy, it is yourself Meenister – I thought it was the hounds of hell coming for me!" The poor lady was quite shaken.

Life on the croft was a pretty tranquil one and the sound of a motorbike at close quarters was quite a shock to her normally serene lifestyle.

"Go in and take a seat Meenister while I go and get ma teeth." Mrs MacKinnon said, still holding her hand in front of her mouth.

Colin smiled to himself and went into the living room and took a seat by a welcoming peat fire.

Before he knew it Mrs MacKinnon came back in

and apologised, "Sorry about that Meenister but I only put my teeth in when I have visitors, and on the Sabbath, of course."

"Don't worry yourself Mrs MacKinnon, the good book tells us, "*Those who guard their mouths and their tongues keep themselves from calamity.'* That's in Proverbs chapter 21 at verse 23, so you should be safe from calamity for quite a while, Mrs MacKinnon!" Colin said with a smile.

"Well, that's good news to be sure Meenister, one lump or two?"
Colin was taken off-guard, "Sorry?"
"Sugar, one lump or two?" Mrs MacKinnon repeated. "My sister was over from Canada last month and brought me a box of fancy sugar lumps. So, one lump or two?"
"Oh, one lump for me please Mrs MacKinnon."

In just a few minutes she came back with a tray on which sat a china teapot, 2 bone china cups, a tray of pancakes, homemade butter with gooseberry jam and a bowl of brown sugar lumps, which she laid on a small table beside him, it wouldn't have looked out of place in a top London restaurant.

This was the traditional kind of highland hospitality he was getting used to (except for the sugar lumps) during his pastoral visits, a custom he thoroughly approved of.

"Help yourself Meenister, you'll be needing to keep your strength up for thon motor bi-cycle that you ride around on.
I don't know whatever is wrong with a horse and cart, it was good enough for our fathers and their fathers too!"
Colin couldn't envisage himself riding around the island on a horse and cart. His idea of real 'horsepower' was a motorbike going at full speed!

As they sat and chatted, Colin was fascinated to hear that Mrs MacKinnon had been a 'lookout' for the military during the Second World War.

Because of her croft's setting, she had a clear view across miles of the Atlantic and could report any suspicious marine activity, such as German ships, in the area.

"Gosh, that must have been exciting for you!" Colin enthused. "Did you ever see any German boats?"

"Oh yes, and submarines too as they surfaced thinking they were out of sight from all civilization."

"Aye, but they didn't reckon on *you*, Mrs MacKinnon!"

"Och, it was little enough to do. An Army Officer and a soldier came across the hill one day, *the road wasn't finished then,* and gave me a 'glass' *(a telescope)* a notebook and a radio with instructions to look out every 4 hours and report back.

I never did find out who I was reporting back to," said Mrs MacKinnon. "It could have been that nice Mr Churchill himself for all I know!"

Colin smiled at the humility of this unsung hero.

Who knows how many lives she saved through her vigilance?

"Did they ever send you a medal Mrs MacKinnon?" Colin asked.

"A medal! What on earth would I do with a medal, Meenister? But I did get a nice letter from thon Mr Atlee. I'm not sure where I put it, or I would show you. It'll be in a drawer somewhere."

Colin was not in the least surprised that she couldn't find it, her modesty was refreshing. Many would have it framed and hung on the wall but not on Rhua, he was slowly finding out that modesty was a common trait among the islanders.

They enjoyed a pleasant hour or so chatting about this and that, when Colin noticed the time on the clock on the mantle-piece. "Good gracious, it's time I was home, my good lady will think I've got lost."

"You'll no' get lost on Rhua Meenister,

whatever road you are on, just keep going and you'll find your way home."

"All roads lead to home, eh Mrs MacKinnon?" Colin smiled.

She understood his play on words but said dryly, "Aye, something like that Meenister, something like that."

They shared a wee prayer, said their farewells and the Rev Colin was soon zooming across the island on his trusty motorbike, heading for home.

His mind wandered to Mrs MacKinnon's fascinating life story when suddenly a huge black cat with a large white spot on its chest, ran across the road and seemed to launch itself at him, causing him to swerve into a stack of hay at the roadside.

He got quite a fright and sat there on the road with his head spinning.
His first thought was, *"I hope the bike's okay!"*

As he tried to stand up he immediately felt dizzy and toppled over into the hay.

A loud droning sound was getting louder and louder and then he heard a voice saying, "That's an unusual place to take a nap Meenister!" It was Donnie MacSween on his Massey tractor.

"Are you alright in there?" Donnie asked.

"Yes, but how's the bike Donnie?" Colin shouted.

"It looks okay from here, you were lucky to land in the hay and not the field, Lachie John's bull is on the prowl just now," Donnie said with a laugh.

"And how did you manage to come off of your motor bi-cycle on this strait stretch of road?" Donnie asked, "Were you at the Communion wine?"

"No, Donnie, it was a huge black cat! It ran straight at me!"

Donnie froze as a shiver ran down his spine.

"A..a.. black cat, you say?" A look of dread came over his face, "Are you sure it was black?"

"Yes, of course I'm sure! And it had a large white spot on its chest."

"Oh mercy, may the good Lord preserve us!" said Donnie.

Colin managed to disentangle himself from the hay stack, and as he was brushing the hay from his jacket, he looked over at Donnie and saw that he had gone visibly pale. "Goodness me Donnie, whatever is the matter?"
"It's …er… nothing… yes nothing, Meenister."

Donnie's shaking was becoming more obvious, as was the tremble in his voice.
"Come on Donnie, what is it?"
"Well, it's just that.. er …. the black cat is bad luck. No-one on the island would have a black cat – except…."
"Except who??" Colin persisted.
"Except the 'Cailleach Dhu' …the black witch!"

"There is always trouble when that cat is seen. It hasn't been seen for a long time, but where the cat is, the Cailleach Dhu is never far away!" Donnie looked around with fear in his eyes.

"Some say that she _is_ the black cat, changing her appearance at will. We call the cat the '*càt sith*' (*caat-shee*). It's a herald of trouble and bad luck! You mark my words, there'll be misfortune for sure!" and he turned his Massey around and fled home as fast as the old tractor would take him.

When he got back to his Croft, Donnie jammed a chair behind the door, closed the curtains and poured himself a very large dram.

Colin stood for a few moments wondering how a cat could put such fear into the heart of Donnie MacSween, a hardy Island character.

As Colin stood rubbing his head, a crowd of 3 locals had gathered at the scene of the crash.

"Did you take a dram with your porridge this morning Meenister?" one said, much to the amusement of his pals.

"No, I did not!" Colin answered. He was about to tell them about the cat but after Donnie's reaction, he thought better of it. "I must have been daydreaming."

"Thinking about next Sunday's Sermon I expect, eh Meenister?" said the more vocal of the three bystanders. Once more the other two spectators laughed at their friends' great wit.

"Aye, that will be it Lachie," Colin replied, conscious that his accent was becoming more like the locals by the week.

Colin struggled to lift his motorbike as the three stood and watched. "Are you not going to give me a hand here, boys?" Colin asked.

"Oh, aye, of course Meenister. Come on lads give the Meenister a hand, look lively now!" Lachie said as he stood back and watched as the other two helped Colin lift his bike upright.

Colin inspected his bike for damage but there were only a few small scratches and stalks of hay stuck in the spokes and engine areas.

Before long, he was on his way back to the Manse.

When he got home, Lorna helped him off with his heavy motorbike jacket and she could feel that he was shaking.

"Colin, you're shaking, are you okay?" Colin related all that had happened, except the bit about the black cat. He knew that being a native of Rhua Lorna was susceptible to thinking deeply about such superstitions, but he also knew that she had a gift for sensing when he was holding something back.

"What *else* happened?" she asked, knowing fine well that Colin was telling the truth, but not the whole truth.

"It's no use sweetheart, I can't keep anything from you can I?"

Lorna smiled "It's your own fault for marrying an Island girl who has the '*gift*'!"

"Okay then, there *is* something else. There was a huge black cat, it ran at me and knocked me off my motorbike, but I'm okay."

Lorna went as white as a sheet. "A black cat, did it have a white patch on its chest?

"Yes, that was it, but it was just a cat darling, nothing to worry about."

Lorna stared into space and asked again, "Are you sure it was a *black* cat?" and she emphasized the world '*black.*'

It didn't matter if it was a normal cat, but a *black* cat, well, that was a different story.

"Yes it was, but ...." Colin was stopped from finishing his sentence.

"There are no buts, Colin," Lorna said. "It was black!"

"But....." Colin was stopped in his tracks again.

"You don't understand! There are *no* black cats on the island, not one. If you saw a black cat then it can only mean one thing - the Cailleach Dhu is back on Rhua! And if that is so, then may the Lord have mercy on us!"

Lorna was now shaking, she was deeply affected by such things and Colin was beginning to see just how much they troubled her.

He put his arms around her. "Now don't be worrying sweetheart, our God is more powerful than any dark force that may attack us.

The 23rd Psalm tells us, *'Even though I walk through the valley of the shadow of death, I will fear no evil, for you are with me.'*

"I know you're right Colin but there are many things which city folk just don't understand. Their lives are surrounded by noise and stresses and strains which do not affect us up here in the Islands.

We live close to nature and we use our senses, our intuition and gifts which are handed down to us from our ancestors. The air is thinner here and we 'see' things, 'feel' things and are more aware of the many forces which are all around us.

Most of those forces are for good but there are a number of evil forces which plague the lives of the people, animals and the land on which we live. We are taught to be cautious from an early age, to be vigilant and on our guard from these dark forces – and it has been so for many centuries. Those who have gone before have passed on their great wisdom, gleaned from *their* forefathers and have handed down that wisdom to us, here, today.

There are both good *and* dark forces all around us, but your people have lost the *gift* of seeing them."

Colin was lost for words, which wasn't like him, but he knew that Lorna was speaking the truth with a wisdom which was far beyond her years. "Gosh, I'd never thought of it in that way, but of course you are right. Perhaps if we..." Colin was interrupted by the telephone ringing.

"Hello, who's calling?" Colin asked.

"It's me, Meenister, Mrs MacAlister's daughter Aileen, speaking,"

"Oh, hello Aileen, how is your mother keeping?"

"I'm afraid she isn't well Meenister, not well at all."

"Oh dear, I am so sorry to hear that - you will have called Doctor Livingstone I presume?"

"No, it's not a doctor that she needs, it's yourself she is calling for!" Aileen MacAlister was becoming increasingly distressed.

"What's happened, Aileen?"

"Mother was putting out the washing when suddenly a large black cat came out of nowhere, it knocked her over and the clothes pole fell on her head and knocked her out for a few minutes. She is convinced that it was the '*càt sith*,' the Cailleach Dhu's cat, and has locked herself in her bedroom and won't come out until the Meenister puts up a prayer!"

A few minutes earlier Colin might have dismissed Mrs MacAlister's fear as irrational but after hearing Lorna's wise words and seeing how frightened she was, he said, "Tell your mother I'll be right over - and you'd better phone Dr Livingstone to take a look at mum's head, oh and Aileen, put the kettle on."

When Colin reached the MacAlister's croft, Aileen was waiting at the door. "How is your mother now, Aileen? Has she calmed down at all?"

"She is still in her bedroom Meenister and won't open the door until you arrive." Aileen led Colin through the hallway to the bedroom door.

"It's only me, Mrs MacAlister, the Minister," Colin shouted through the bedroom door.

"You can come out now, the cat has gone."

"It's not the cat that worries me, it's the Cailleach Dhu who is sure to be close by." Mrs McAlister sounded terrified. "Will you put up a blessing on us, Meenister? It's the only thing that will save us from her dark powers."

Colin could sense the fear in her voice so in order to calm her down he said, "Of course I will, but it would be more effective if we prayed together, so why not come out and we will sit and ask for God's protection?"

Mrs MacAlister cautiously opened the bedroom door. Looking left and right as she made her way to the living room.

She sat between her daughter and the Meenister, and they held hands as Colin prayed for protection from all dark and evil forces.

Just as they finished their prayer, there was a knock at the door and a dishevelled looking Dr. Livingstone appeared. "Hello! God, the midgies are bad the day!" he said cheerily, completely ruining the solemn atmosphere in the room. "Sorry I'm a bit late but I was up all night helping Jenny Ferguson's Morag who was having a breach birth, I didn't get to bed until five o'clock this morning!"

Colin froze at the thought of Jenny's daughter having her personal problems being discussed quite so openly.
"I had to hold her down to stop her thrashing about, and she gave me a nasty kick!"

"I say Doctor, I think that's quite enough about Jenny Ferguson's daughter! Very bad taste!"
Everyone in the room laughed, except Colin.

Dr. Livingstone laughed the loudest saying, "Daughter? Morag is Jenny's prize cow! It's easily seen that you're a Glasgow keelie."
Colin turned the colour of a beetroot and stuttered, "Oh, I see. Gosh... I mean... well... how was I...er..."
Mrs MacAlister took pity on Colin and came to the rescue, "Don't be worrying yourself

Meenister, it's an easy mistake to make, how were you to know that Jenny Ferguson's daughter is called Daisy!"

The room erupted again, and poor Colin didn't know where to look.

"Aileen, away and make us a wee cup of tea, and make sure the Meenister's is a strong one." Mrs MacAlister said and winked at her daughter.

"Okay mother," said Aileen as she went through to the scullery.

Dr. Livingstone saw the wink and knew that a dram would be put into the Meenister's tea.

Not being one to shy away from taking a dram, he sat down and made himself very much at home, hoping that with any luck there might a few more drams on offer if he were to stretch things out.

"I like my tea strong too Aileen." He shouted through to the kitchen. As the Doctor sat back and crossed his legs Colin noticed that although he had his tweed trousers on, his blue striped pyjama trousers were sticking out at the turn-ups. He had just got up and dressed in haste.

Dr. Livingstone then took out a packet of Woodbine cigarettes and lit one up, puffing a large cloud of smoke across the room.
Colin was taken aback and asked, "Doctor, should you be smoking, you being a Doctor, is it not bad for your health?"
"Och," said Doctor Livingstone, "if the cigarettes don't get you, the midgies will!" and expelled another puff of smoke into the room.

After two or three cups of tea, with their 'spiritual' content, Colin was in good form. He was over his embarrassment about the 'Morag' business and enjoying the Doctor's company very much.
"That's a lovely cup of tea," he said to Aileen. "What is it called?"
Aileen wasn't sure what to say but in a flash of inspiration she said, "It's called Mountain Dew," which brought a smile to the company.

"That's a strange name for tea, but whatever it's called, it's lovely, I'll have to ask Lorna to get some in, is there any chance of another cup, Aileen?"

*

During Colin's visit to Mrs MacAlister's croft, there had been a number of phone calls to the Manse regarding a large black cat that has seen around the island.

Lorna had taken the calls and left several notes beside the phone for Colin when he returned home. She had a deep feeling of foreboding as she sat waiting, worrying, and growing ever anxious as she watched the clock.

'Something evil is out and about on the island,' she thought to herself. *'I hope nothing has happened to Colin, Meenisters are prone to Cailleach Dhu's malevolent mischief making.'*

She recalled the last time the Cailleach Dhu had visited Rhua and how the Reverend McCrimmond, the Free church Minister, had been walking home after visiting one of his parishioners late one evening and was attacked by a very large black cat. He was knocked over, hit his head on the road and laid unconscious for a number of hours. Dr Livingstone was worried that he might have brain damage but when he came round, the first thing he asked for was a dram, so they knew he was his old self again.

Or the time Reverend McCrimmond was heading home one evening after another pastoral visit and was suddenly overpowered by a band of unknown ruffians who held him down and poured whisky down his throat – or at least that was his story – causing him to wander around the island until he was found laid out on the Machair, within staggering distance from the Bothan."

Colin smiled.

"He said it was done to besmirch his good name. It was never explained, but Reverend McCrimmond thought he saw two glowing eyes from a large black cat staring at him through the dark while he was lying on the ground unable to stand up, due to some strange power that held him down.

We couldn't work out how he could have seen that the cat was black, seeing as the incident took place in the middle of the night.

There were those who thought that Reverend McCrimmond's strange encounters were the result of taking too much 'hospitality' while visiting his flock, but being a man of the cloth, no-one was willing to challenge his accounts of what took place on those dark nights.

But there had been a number of other incidents which Lorna knew to be strange and disturbing.

On one occasion, she had sensed the close presence of the Cailleach Dhu, although she couldn't see her, and could still remember the fear which had run through her body during that encounter, it was a fear that she didn't want to experience again, if it could be at all avoided.

*

On his return to the Manse, Lorna updated Colin with the phone calls she had received while he was out.

"My goodness, the black cat has been busy!" Colin said. "What do you *really* make of this 'black cat' business, sweetheart?" he asked Lorna.

She sat for a few moments trying to be open minded and rational but with her upbringing and her own gift of the second sight, she knew that there was a dark presence hanging over Rhua.

"I know some will say it's silly superstition, but I feel that a dark spirit is moving around the island just now. From the tales of our ancestors, the Cailleach Dhu has been coming here for centuries and I have felt her presence on more than one occasion, so I don't take these latest sightings lightly."

Colin could see that Lorna was getting anxious again, so he said brightly, "Ok sweetheart. I'll tell you what, if you pass me the phone messages, I'll have a look through them and then go out and do a bit of visiting to see if we can get to the bottom of this, then we can plan what's best to do next. How about a cup of tea and a custard cream before I go?"

Lorna put the kettle on while Colin read through the notes.

He saw that there had been six phone calls while he had been out visiting Mrs MacAlister. All six had seen a black cat just prior to some calamitous misfortune taking place.

Colin was becoming more puzzled as he sat trying to understand what was going on. Was it just superstitious nonsense? Had someone seen a black cat and now people were seeing black cats everywhere? Or was it something more sinister? Lorna certainly took it seriously and she wasn't one to have the wool pulled over her eyes easily, so he decided to pay a visit to those who had phoned and get a better idea of this whole strange business.

Fortified by a cup of tea and two custard creams, Colin drove off, leaving Lorna at home, worrying about him. He was naïve in these matters, and she feared for his safety.

As she pondered how she could help Colin, she remembered the mysterious woman who lived on the far side of the island called, 'Brigid Bana bhuidseach' (*pronounced, 'Bana-vootsch-och' – say it quickly*) - meaning 'Brigid the Witch.'
Perhaps she could help. Most people, with any sense, kept their distance from her.

Her appearance was very striking, she was tall with bright green eyes, flame red hair and pale skin and was said to be descended from the legendary Irish Tuath Dé, the Tribe of the Gods, who were known for their war painted faces and bright red hair.
 No one knew where she came from, but she certainly spoke with an Irish brogue and her Gaelic was different to that of the locals. Her strange appearance convinced the locals that whoever she was, she was very different from them.

The parents, grandparents and great grandparents all spoke of a tall red haired woman living in a remote part of the island. If that were true, then it would mean Brigid had been around Rhua for over 500 hundred years, maybe more!

Lorna decided to give her a visit and hoped she would receive a friendly welcome.

It was known that anyone who strayed too close to Brigid's wee croft was invariably chased by her dog, a large hairy, Irish wolf-hound called Connor, the size of a bear, with blazing red eyes, if the stories were to be believed.

Colin was away on his motorbike, so the car was in the garage. After writing a short note to Colin saying she had popped out to visit a friend who might be able to help (the good Lord would understand). She placed a custard cream biscuit on the note and drove off to Brigid's croft.

Colin spent the afternoon visiting the callers, each had a similar tale to tell. A big black cat had appeared, followed by an incident or accident.

Not all of the occurrences were life threatening, but all of the witnesses were left badly shaken.

The last of his visits had been to Mr and Mrs Campbell's secluded croft. It was surrounded by trees, and unless you ventured into the woods you would go right past it at the road end and not know it was there.

The croft saw hardly any sunshine because of its location among the trees and Colin felt uncomfortable as he parked up his motorbike and walked over to the door where Mrs Campbell, a dark, sullen woman was waiting for him.

"It's yourself Meenister, I thought you would have been sooner, but I suppose we're not important enough," she said.

"Yes, I'm sorry but I er… got lost. There are plenty of wee roads and junctions but no signposts." He said in his defence.

"When you've been here as long as we have you don't need signposts. Oh well, you may as well come in now you're here."

The croft was dark inside and Colin had to peer in order to see his way, even though he was following Mrs Campbell. He made out a dark figure in the corner, it was Mr Campbell sitting in an armchair.

As Colin's eyes got used to the dimness, he saw that he had a large glass of what looked like whisky, in his hand.

"Come away in Meenister" Mr Campbell said in a friendly tone. Colin's spirit brightened.

"Is that you Mr Campbell?" Colin said before realising that it was a daft question.

"Aye, it's myself Meenister, take a seat. Molly, get the Meenister a dram."

"Not for me thank you," Colin said. "I'm on the motorbike, better not get arrested for drunk in charge of a motorbike, eh Mrs Campbell? Maybe a cup of coffee if you don't mind."

"We don't hold with coffee in this house, so it'll be tea." And she walked through to the kitchen.

"Never mind the good lady, Meenister, she's not a well woman I'm afraid. She enjoys ill health."

"Oh dear, I'm so sorry to hear that Mr Campbell."

"Call me Duncan, I've been called worse!" he laughed out loud and took another gulp from his glass.

"Okay thank you. Duncan, what's all this about a black cat?"

"Aye, it's a strange business right enough. Molly was splitting logs outside….."

Colin interrupted, "Sorry, your wife was splitting logs?"

"Oh yes, I'm not able to do anything physical due to my condition."

"Oh, right, I'm sorry, please carry on."

"Well as I was saying, Molly was outside when an elderly old Cailleach (*old lady*) came into the yard, with a black cat sitting across her shoulders. She gave Molly a real fright as she wasn't there one minute and then next minute – she was! If you get my drift."

Colin wasn't sure that he did, but simply said, "Oh, right."

Duncan continued with his story.

"Molly had said to the Cailleach, "*We don't want any lucky white heather – or pegs, thank you very much!*" And then the Cailleach walked slowly over to Molly who feared that she would be attacked, or worse, perhaps she might have a curse put upon her!"

"Oh dear!" Colin said, "quite an experience for your good lady, is she alright?"

"She is – and it's thanks to the good Lord that she was saved from the old witch."

"What makes you say she was a witch?" Colin was beginning to think that perhaps there was more to this encounter than meets the eye.

"Well, because the weather is so hot just now, and as we never have any visitors, Molly was wearing an old vest of mine to cut the logs, ready for the winter. It gives her more dexterity with swinging the axe," explained Duncan.

Colin smiled and asked, "And how do you mean that she was *saved by the good Lord*?"

"Well, when the Cailleach came close and saw that Molly was wearing a gold cross around her neck – *it was her dear late mother's* – the Cailleach let out a mighty scream, covered her eyes and fled like a scalded cat, shouting curses as she vanished into the woods."

Colin sat for a few moments processing all he had heard.

"I see, so the cross had frightened the old lady away?"

"Aye Meenister, did I not just say so?" Duncan replied.

"Mmm, I wonder…." Colin said softly, his mind was working overtime, he had the seeds of a plan.

He jumped up and made for the door just as Molly Campbell was coming in with a tray of scones, teapot and three of their best china cups. "Is that you leaving, Meenister? And after I've gone to all the bother of making some tea!" Molly was not best pleased.

"My apologies Mrs Campbell but I have some important business to deal with but thank you for your help. Oh, and I am pleased that you are unharmed."

She looked over at her husband and said, "Whatever does he mean, 'pleased I am unharmed.' What have you been saying to the Meenister?"

"I told him about the old Cailleach's visit."

"I thought I told you never to tell a soul about that!"

"Don't worry Mrs Campbell, your ordeal is safe with me, now I have to go," and he hurried out of the croft.

"Meenister's today!" she said shaking her head. "Mr McCrimmond would never have left without his dram, indeed, sometimes we couldn't get him to leave at all!" and she walked back to the kitchen, mumbling under her breath.

Colin spent the next hour or so visiting the Elders, talking things through with them and listening to their thoughts and suggestions.

*

Across the island at Brigid's small croft, Lorna had managed to negotiate her way past the big hairy hound, Connor, which was tied to a post. To Lorna's surprise (and relief) the dog remained passive but its blazing red eyes followed her as she walked cross the yard.

Just as she was about to knock on the door it opened slowly and there stood 'Brigid the Witch'. "Don't worry about Connor, he's been expecting you. Please come in." she said.

This was not their first meeting and there was a feeling of mutual trust and respect between them. Brigid knew that Lorna had the 'gift of the second sight' and Lorna was aware that Brigid was a 'glic boireannach' (a 'wise woman') who had gifts and powers far deeper and stronger than Lorna could ever imagine.

The croft was like a time capsule. It was a single storey with just one room and had an earthen floor and only one window. The bed was over to one end of the room where the cows and the chickens would have been kept in times past.

It also had a central hearth without a chimney, just a hole in the roof to allow the smoke to rise out of the croft.

The interior walls of the dark croft were covered with shelves on which numerous jars stood full of goodness knows what, and there were wall hanging cloths with signs and symbols that Lorna had never seen before. As her eyes were adjusting to the gloom she saw shadows darting this way and that, or was it her imagination?

In the corner of the room she saw two small green lights shining brightly, Lorna jumped as they blinked and when she looked closer she realised that a pure white cat with bright emerald green eyes was staring up at her.
Lorna had seen some of these old 'black houses' before as there were still a few dotted around the island, but most were now in ruins.

Brigid was what some might call an 'old soul.' She was wise and knowledgeable in the 'old ways,' and yet she seemed well informed in what was going on outside of the walls of her remote croft.
"How is your husband, the Minister, settling in?" Brigid asked. Lorna was surprised that she

knew about Colin as she was never seen out and about the island. She wondered how she was able to keep up with the business of the outside world.

"He is well, thank you – and that brings me to why I am here."

"Yes, of course…" Brigid said knowingly.

Lorna explained her worries about the presence of the Cailleach Dhu on the island and her husband's vulnerability as a Minister, and said that she would appreciate any help or advice that Brigid could offer.

Brigid listened carefully and then said that the Cailleach Dhu was actually her older sister and their mother had been Queen Oonagh, queen of an ancient Irish kingdom a long time ago.

Being the eldest, her sister was to succeed their mother as queen, on her death, but because of her fondness for the dark side, she was overlooked, and Brigid was chosen over her.

They had a violent quarrel and the Cailleach Dhu had put a curse on Brigid who, in order to break the curse, travelled across water and made her home on the first island she came to, which, due to the vagaries of the wind, the tides, and perhaps fate, was Rhua.

Her sister was banished from the kingdom and now roamed the world, practicing her dark art as it suited her.

They hadn't spoken for many long years, she said, Lorna didn't like to ask just how many years!

"Would it be possible for you to talk to your sister and convince her to leave Rhua? She might listen to you," Lorna asked.

"She won't listen to me, but perhaps there *is* something I can do."

They talked for an hour or so and a kind of plan was put together. It was more of an outline of a plan really, as much depended on how things went on the night.

When Lorna got home, she could see that Colin's motorbike was at the side of the house and she knew that he would have seen her note lying on the kitchen table – and guessed that the custard cream would be gone.

He had made a few stop-offs on the way home and a plan was beginning to form in his head, now he wanted to speak to Lorna for her thoughts.

"Well, how did you get on?" Lorna asked.

"Great, but before we start, how about putting the kettle on and I'll get the custard creams?" Colin suggested.

"A great idea!" Lorna agreed.

They sat at the kitchen table with their tea and biscuits and talked over all that they had discovered on their separate visits.

Colin explained how Mrs Campbell's cross had frightened the Cailleach Dhu away and they both agreed that was significant.

He was intrigued to hear how Lorna had got on with her friend.

She explained who she had *really* visited, Brigid the Witch.

Colin was fearful. "Oh, Lorna was that not dangerous?"

"Don't be worrying sweetheart, I've met her before and was on my guard." She went through all that she and Brigid had talked about.

"You mean they are sisters?" Colin was beginning to get excited. "I think we're on to something!"

"Absolutely Colin – and there's even more.

She told me that her sister's real name is Fionnuala, *'Cailleach Dhu'* is just a name that we call her, it means, *the old black witch.*"

Lorna went on to tell him more of her conversation with Brigid and how they were the daughters of a Queen of an ancient Irish Kingdom.

.

Colin was finding all the talk of witches, curses and ancient Irish kingdoms hard to deal with. He had always thought of those kinds of things as being just superstitious nonsense believed by the vulnerable and susceptible, but he knew that Lorna was certainly neither of those.

"That's very interesting," Colin said. "But before we can do anything, we have to find her and I don't suppose Brigid told you where she is?"

"Well, actually – she did!" said Lorna.

"You mean she...?" Colin was lost for words. "Yes, she told me that she can get in touch with her, but we have to be very careful, she is an extremely dangerous person to cross."

"Well, we'll just have to be careful then. Well done you, for getting all that information!" Colin was impressed by his lovely wife's detective work.

"Och, what can I say?" she gave a look of feigned embarrassment and said, "We make a good team, don't we Colin?"

"We certainly do sweetheart, we certainly do. With your beauty and my brains, we could go far!" He said cheekily.

"Hey! Watch it!" Lorna laughed and picked up Colin's half munched custard cream, popped it into her mouth and walked out of the kitchen.

Colin smiled and went through to his study to give some thought on where to go from here.

In order to put a plan together, he wrote down his own thoughts and the ideas that the Elders had suggested. On a separate sheet he noted all that Lorna had gleaned from Brigid the Witch.

'I'm sure there is a plan to be found in here…. Mmm,' he said to himself as he scanned his notes.

He took a few moments in prayer, asking for guidance and the eyes to see a way ahead.

On opening his eyes, he remembered the incident with Mrs Campbell when she was cutting up logs at her croft.

"Of course – the cross!" he said out loud. "That's

where to start!" It was the prompt he needed to kick-start his mind into action.

Lorna had come through with a cup of tea and could see Colin busy writing. "How are you getting on sweetheart?" she asked him.

"Great, take a seat and I'll run it past you, and perhaps we can fine-tune it together."

For the next half an hour or so they sat chatting excitedly as a plan revealed itself.

"It's a great plan," Lorna said with a smile.

"Aye, but do you think it will work?" Colin replied.

"I'm quite sure it will... I think!" Lorna had faith in their plan but was aware of the dangers too.

"Brigid said that the Cailleach Dhu was just getting started and the worst was yet to come – unless she is stopped!"

"And that's exactly what we must do! We have

our separate parts to play and so long as we stick to the plan I'm sure the good Lord will carry us through and banish the old witch from Rhua forever.

We must put our faith in Him sweetheart, you know what the good book says, "*Commit thy works unto the Lord, and thy thoughts shall succeed.*" (Proverbs 16 : 3)

"Okay then," Colin continued. "I'll go back to the Elders and fill them in with the plan. I could be some time, so don't wait up for me, sweetheart.

With that, Colin gave Lorna a kiss on the cheek and sped off to update the Elders.

Colin was late home as expected, but he and the Elders had been busy putting the plan together and fine tuning it until they were all happy with their own part. It just depended how it would work out in practice.

Colin woke early the next morning, Sunday, with a feeling of excitement mixed with apprehension. He turned over to speak to Lorna but saw that she was not there. He heard noises coming from the kitchen and wandered through to see her cooking up a breakfast of Ham *(bacon)* and eggs.

"What a wonderful sight for a man to wake up to - his wife making a hearty breakfast for him!"

"Don't be expecting this every morning, now!" replied Lorna. "I just thought that as we have such a busy day, we should go out with a good breakfast inside us."

There was a full house at the morning service. People were coming from all over the island to hear him preach. His sermons were understandable and relatable, with no heavy theological terminology. His theme was taken from 1st Corinthians 1 : 18, *'The Cross seems foolish to those who don't believe, but for those of us who <u>do</u> believe, the Cross is the very Power of God.'*

As one lady was heard to say, *"He has the gift of the preaching to be sure. He always challenges me with something to think about in my own daily life of faith."*

To all outward appearance, it was a normal Sunday morning, but Colin and Lorna knew all that lay ahead, and there would be dark and dangerous undertakings before the night was out.

After the last Psalm was sung and the Benediction pronounced, Colin asked the Elders to remain behind. They knew that this would be a final pep talk before their meeting at the Fairy Well just before sunset, that time when day turns into night and light turns into darkness.

They met in the vestry and Colin went over the plan for later in the day once more.

He knew he could trust every one of them. These were men of faith and of courage. Some of them had served in the Royal Navy during both Great Wars and had seen their ships torpedoed, shipmates burned alive and others drowning, shouting for help as their ship sunk slowly beneath the waves.

Others had been called up to serve in various Regiments, including the 51st and 52nd Highland

Divisions, experiencing and enduring the horrors of the Somme, St Valery, the dreadful trenches, gas attacks and much more. Many still suffered from the memories of losing good friends and family members and having to leave them lying in a foreign country far from their beloved Island.

He knew that they would be tested to the limit before nightfall, and he had no doubt of their courage and loyalty in adversity.

One of the Elders, with the grand name of Robert Hay MacDonald, had brought a number of Rowan tree branches from his estate, at Colin's request, and they set about their business for the next hour or so.

After some discussion, they spent time in prayer. Colin prayed for each one of them by name, asking for God's protection from what lay ahead.

He was taken aback when the senior elder, Teàrlach (Charles) McKinnon, finished off the prayer by praying, "Lord, watch over our

Meenister, and give him your strength and protection as he faces the dark forces of evil, later this very day."

Colin was moved and a tear ran down his cheek as he closed the meeting with a reading from the prophet Isaiah ~ *"Fear not, for I am with you ; do not be dismayed, for I am your God; I will strengthen you, I will help you, I will uphold you with my righteous right hand." (Isaiah 41 : 10)* – and they all said, 'Amen.'

They were now ready for whatever lay ahead, or at least, as ready as they could be.

That evening, as the light was beginning to fade, Brigid and her sister, the Cailleach Dhu, who was clutching her black cat, were standing by the Fairy Well, just as Brigid and Lorna had discussed.

The Cailleach Dhu wasn't best pleased at being summoned to a meeting and was vehemently cursing her sister Brigid, so much so that she hadn't noticed the Elders emerging slowly from the trees, surrounding her at the well.

Each of them held up high a wooden cross (*made of Rowan wood, known for its mystical qualities*) in their right hand and a Bible in their left.

As darkness began to fall, they gradually closed in on the old witch, surrounding her on every side.

Colin came forward and he too held high his cross in one hand and a bible in the other and called out, *"The Lord will strike down all those who practice evil and witchcraft and they will burn like the furnace burns the chaff. No evil doer will be spared, and their spells and curses will not save them from the Almighty's wrath. For everyone who has been born again of God shall overcome all that is evil. No witch can touch them, no spell will harm them, the Lord our God will lift them up to glory on the last day, and the Angels will sing their halleluiah's. Be gone evil one, be gone!"*

All the Elders echoed the call, chanting, "Be gone evil one, be gone!" - holding up the wooden crosses that they had made from the

Rowan branches that afternoon, in the church hall, with the Minister.

Brigid the Witch chanted a verse from an ancient manuscript which was said to exorcise dark powers.

Lorna read a passage from the Bible, *"The Lord is faithful, and He will strengthen you and protect you from the evil one."(2nd Thessalonians Chapter 3, verse 3).*

The Cailleach Dhu spat and cursed but it was no use, the power against her was too much for her to bear and she fell to the ground and gave out an almighty scream, which was followed by bright flash of lightening and then....... an eerie silence.

It was almost dark, and difficult to see, but the loud sound of bird wings flapping was heard, or at least that is what it sounded like.

A number of Elders were sure they saw two large Ravens flying up and out to sea.

As their eyes got used to the dark, they could see no sign of the Cailleach Dhu or her cat, only her black cloak lying on the ground. Brigid gathered it up and made her way over to speak to Lorna, they hugged and she walked away into the night.

The Elders were drained, so were Colin and Lorna but they were jubilant too. "We did it, she's gone!" shouted one elder and the others cheered. Another said loudly, "The power of the cross!" Wasn't that just what you were saying in your sermon this morning Meenister!?"

"That's right Alistair, there is power in the cross, you've seen it for yourselves this very night," Colin said with great conviction.

"Now remember, this is never to be spoken of, not to your family or friends or to anyone. If anybody asks what our meeting was about, simply say that it was a Kirk Session meeting to discuss fundraising for a new roof."

They all nodded and chatted among themselves with great excitement, and all agreed that a very large dram was in order, even though it was the Sabbath. 'Himself' (The Good Lord) would understand.

Lorna ran over to Colin, hugged him and said, "Oh Colin, you were wonderful!"

"It wasn't just me sweetheart, we all played our part, and well done *you* for getting Brigid onside and persuading her to lure her sister to a meeting. I saw her speaking to you just now, what did she have to say?"

"She said that it was unlikely that the Cailleach Dhu would ever come back to Rhua – her dark powers were so weakened by such a show of Faith that life would be too difficult for her here. She's gone, thank God!" Lorna said.

"Yes sweetheart, exactly that," said Colin, "We must thank God!"

By this time, the daylight had gone completely, and the night was as black as a Bible.

*

The last word goes to Lachlan *'the seer'* MacÀidh (Lachie McKay) late of Eilan Beg, Rhua, aged 111 on the year of his passing into eternal rest.

When asked if he thought the Cailleach Dhu was a witch, he answered ~

"There are many things going on all around us, that only those with the 'sight' can see, and I have seen some very unholy and blasphemous things whenever she was on the Island, dark and dreadful things – I have seen them with my own eyes and trembled.

May the Good Lord, in His mercy, preserve us."

*

Chapter 11

Happy Days are here again…

As in most small communities, secrets don't stay secret for very long, and in time, word of what happened that evening at the Fairy Well got out. Thereafter Colin and that small band of Elders were held in very high esteem by the islanders, even to this very day.

It brought the people of Rhua together in a way that nothing else could have, and a new wave of faith swept through the people.

It became the custom across the island to place a small Rowan or Hawthorn wooden cross above the door of their crofts, to ward off all evil.

Life on Rhua was good again.

Colin's congregation grew week by week – and soon Lorna noticed she was putting on weight and feeling queasy in the mornings.
A visit to Dr Killmennie confirmed her suspicions that she was expecting a baby.

The community were delighted at the good news and Lorna and Colin received many handmade cards (*in handmade envelopes*) wishing the three of them well.

In time, Lorna gave birth to a beautiful wee girl, and they called her Fiona.

In the following years Lorna and Colin were blessed with two more children, two boys, Iain and Fionnlagh (Finlay).

Fiona grew up to be the very image of her mother, qualifying as a Teacher and taking up a post in Rhua's newly built school, fulfilling her own mother's childhood dreams.

Iain had the wanderlust in him and he joined the Royal Navy, travelling around the world before going to the Edinburgh Theological Seminary to study Divinity, and was later Ordained as a Minister in the Free Church.

Finlay became a social worker and now works

in and around the Western Islands, focusing on the many social issues associated with living on a remote Island.

Colin and Lorna were content and justifiably proud of their children.

To complete the happy family, one of the parishioners gave them a puppy, and they called him Rory (Ruaridh - *due to his deep red coat*), which gave them many happy years of love, fun and enjoyment, much to the delight of the children and the grandchildren.

And - in the tradition of all good Tales,
they all lived happily ever after.

THE END.

"Isn't it wonderful to know that

some of the best things of our lives

are yet to happen...?"

I hope you enjoyed my Trilogy of Books and who knows – the Reverend Colin and Lorna and his family, might appear in more exploits in the future.

And if you should spot a 'spin-off' book called ~ 'PC Bookem's Casebook' by Iain MacGillivray (my mother's 'maiden name') then only you and I will know who wrote it – but don't tell anyone else!

But until then…

Take care and keep safe.

Slàinte mhòr agus a h-uile beannachd dhuibh.

Great health and every good blessing to you.

Other titles from this Author
(so far…)

Tales of a Highland Minister
(Book 1)

More Tales of a Highland Minister
(Book 2)

And, of course, this book ~
Even More Tales of a Highland Minister
(Book 3)
*

These books are all available on Amazon.

If you enjoyed these stories, could I ask you to take a few minutes to leave a review on both Facebook and/or Amazon so that others may be encouraged to read and enjoy them too.
Thank you *so* much.

Iain

Front Cover Artwork

'The Sweet Maraig Cottage'

North Harris, Western Isles

Scotland

*

By kind permission of ~

Dona Johnson,
Artist, Isle of Harris,

Contact ~ Art by Dona Isle of Harris

(Facebook page)

Thank you Dona!

*

Also ~ check out LinPin's amazing and unique Scottish artwork at ~ www.linpincrafts.com

·